ISBN 978-0-259-76673-5
PIBN 10824403

This book is a reproduction of an important historical work. Forgotten Books uses state-of-the-art technology to digitally reconstruct the work, preserving the original format whilst repairing imperfections present in the aged copy. In rare cases, an imperfection in the original, such as a blemish or missing page, may be replicated in our edition. We do, however, repair the vast majority of imperfections successfully; any imperfections that remain are intentionally left to preserve the state of such historical works.

1 MONTH OF
FREE
READING

at

www.ForgottenBooks.com

By purchasing this book you are eligible for one month membership to ForgottenBooks.com, giving you unlimited access to our entire collection of over 1,000,000 titles via our web site and mobile apps.

To claim your free month visit:
www.forgottenbooks.com/free824403

English
Français
Deutsche
Italiano
Español
Português

www.forgottenbooks.com

Mythology Photography **Fiction**
Fishing Christianity **Art** Cooking
Essays Buddhism Freemasonry
Medicine **Biology** Music **Ancient
Egypt** Evolution Carpentry Physics
Dance Geology **Mathematics** Fitness
Shakespeare **Folklore** Yoga Marketing
Confidence Immortality Biographies
Poetry **Psychology** Witchcraft
Electronics Chemistry History **Law**
Accounting **Philosophy** Anthropology
Alchemy Drama Quantum Mechanics
Atheism Sexual Health **Ancient History**
Entrepreneurship Languages Sport
Paleontology Needlework Islam
Metaphysics Investment Archaeology
Parenting Statistics Criminology
Motivational

THE

CRADLE

OF THE

DEEP

BY

JOAN LOWELL

Illustrated by KURT WIESE

1929

SIMON AND SCHUSTER
NEW YORK

FIRST PRINTING MARCH 1929, 75,000 COPIES

COPYRIGHT, 1929, BY SIMON AND SCHUSTER, INC.
37 WEST 57 STREET NEW YORK
PRINTED IN U. S. A. BY VAIL-BALLOU PRESS, BINGHAMTON
BOUND BY H. WOLFF EST., N. Y.
DESIGNED BY ANDOR BRAUN

TO

E D W A R D L . B E R N A Y S
AND
H I R A M K E L L Y M O T H E R W E L L
who encouraged me to write this book

TABLE OF CONTENTS

TABLE OF CONTENTS

THE CRADLE OF THE DEEP

T

"I spit a curve in the wind"

"SHE ain't any water rat, ma'm! She's a girl flower, she is, with the tropic heavens fer a hothouse, and the scoldin' of the storm fer her when she's bad. An' she knows all that we sailormen know—all the good—'cause no one of us ever let her hear nothin' else."

It was Old John Henry, one of our sailors, defending me to the wife of an American Consul in an Australian port. She had asked him, as he stood on watch at the gangway, what kind of a "water rat" was the Captain's daughter, living such a rough life among rough men on a schooner. And John Henry, feeling he must uphold the dignity of the Captain's daughter and the genteelness of sailormen, had replied with all the sea poetry he could command.

"But how awful for a girl to be raised on a ship with nothing but men," persisted the woman unconvinced. She hadn't seen me but she had heard the talk of the waterfront and she knew I must be rough, and coarse and low —just awful—raised without the softening feminine influence.

"Awful, hell!" snorted John Henry. "She ain't no damn fool like most women; her Old Man uses a rope's end on her stern often enough to keep the foolishness outen her head."

I was taking it easy, rolled up in the canvas of the mizzen sail which was furled on the mizzen boom. If I hadn't been afraid of women I would have come down to see how different she was from me because I couldn't understand why any one should think it strange that I lived on a ship with no woman to care for me. Hadn't she gone to sea when she was a little girl? I supposed every girl went to sea when she was young for I knew nothing but the sea and strange island ports.

The smell of rotting copra, putrid pearl oysters drying, sandalwood in little bundles piled high on our deck, the fumes from a cargo of guano, and sacks of ivory nuts— these things, the places they came from and the people who brought them to us were the commonplaces of my life. The legends of the sea told me by the sailors on our ship were my fairy tales; the freak storms, the bewildering doldrums in the tropics, and the companionship of old shell-back sailors, the foundation of my experience.

My father's ship, the *Minnie A. Caine,* was a four-masted, windjammer rigged schooner, engaged in the copra and sandalwood trade between the islands of the South Seas and Australia. I couldn't remember when I wasn't on a ship. Born in Berkeley, California—known in the maritime world as "the sea Captain's bedroom"— I was the eleventh child in our family. Four of my

brothers and sisters had died in two years. They called
me the lick of the pan because I was last and not much of
me. No one expected me to grow up, but Father said:

"This is the last one and I'm going to save it. I'll take
it away from the land and let the sea make it the pick of
the puppies." So he took me when I was less than a year
old and I lived on shipboard until I was seventeen, and if
the sea didn't make me the pick of the puppies, at least
it made me the huskiest.

Father brought me up with no creed except fear and
respect for the gods that brew the storms and calms.

As to God Himself, I can say only that in my early life
He and I were on most intimate terms. I had not half the
fear of Him that I had of Father. I felt much closer to
Him because I could discuss many things with Him that
I wouldn't have dared mention to Father. He was my
friend, confidant, and counselor and I always felt that
He approved of everything I did, and if I felt He dis-
approved I would argue until I convinced Him—in my
own mind! Our arguments and discussions took place at
the masthead far above the deck where no one could hear
our private conversations.

Many a time I climbed to the cross-trees of the foremast and had it out with Him. If things had gone well
with me I thanked Him—as for instance, if I managed
to steal an extra hunk of brown sugar from the storeroom
for my oatmeal, without being caught, I thought He was
a good sport and told Him so. But I gave Him hell if He
let *us* get caught in a sudden storm that ripped our sails
or if we were becalmed in the deadly doldrums.

Father was very different—much more concrete, harder
to twist around my finger—more to be feared than God,

in my estimation. I could say anything to God—praise Him, gossip with Him or tell Him to go to the devil, and I did. But in all my years on the ship I heard few ever tell Father to go to the devil and none ever did it twice!

It was from my father that I inherited my love of the sea, the understanding of it, and the courage to face it. The sea was his life and he never wanted any other. How could a boy, born on an old clipper ship lying in far-off Geelong Bay, Australia, expect to do anything but follow the sea, and, if the Wanderlust ruled his blood, certainly he came by it naturally.

My grandfather, Louis Lazzarrevich, was a Montenegrin land owner and my grandmother a beautiful girl of Turkish blood whom Louis Lazzarrevich had married in spite of the Montenegrin hatred of the Turks. Life in Montenegro with a Turkish wife was not so pleasant. Consequently, after the birth of their first child, the young couple, to get away, planned a trip around the world in a sailing ship. In Geelong Bay, Australia, where the ship had put in, my father was born. My grandmother was so ill that her husband took her ashore and told the captain of the clipper ship that they would stay in Australia, and he could pick them up on his return voyage in two years.

Within a week of the time of their landing, my grandfather was accidentally drowned in Geelong Bay. That left my grandmother stranded with two children, my father and his older sister.

Shortly after my grandfather's death, my grandmother met a fascinating German pearl-trader, Captain Wagner. Beautiful women were scarce in Australia in those days, and there has always been a certain affinity between beautiful women and pearls. Moreover Turkish women are fatalistic. So it was not long before the pearl-trader married my grandmother, but, once married, he absolutely refused to have his honeymoon cluttered up with his predecessor's children. As to my grandmother, new love and the pearls outweighed old love and her children—and as I have said before, Turkish women are fatalistic.

So she and her pearl-trader sailed away to the South Seas, and the good Jesuit Fathers took in the unwanted children.

For the first ten years of his life my father endured the confinement, the strict discipline and the soul loneliness of the Jesuit Orphan Asylum, and then the Wanderlust in his blood took hold. Fearing the good Fathers might not understand, and not wishing to hurt their feelings by telling them what he thought of their orphanage, he departed quietly one night without saying goodbye. A few days later when he left Australia on a trading schooner plying between Melbourne and China, that same modesty and diffidence kept him from letting the captain or the crew know he was on board until, when they were out at sea, hunger forced his confession. They whipped him and put him to work, but they couldn't turn back or stop the ship on his account so he got to China.

Then followed eight years' work on traders in the Far East before the boy, now eighteen, sailed into San Francisco Bay, deckhand on a full-rigged English clipper.

San Francisco at that time was only a sheltered harbor with a dock about a block long!

One day a young girl wandered down to the wharf to watch the ships come in. On the clipper ship she saw a handsome, dark-haired young man holystoning the deck. He spoke to her. She had never seen any one like him before. He told her stories of the sea, stories of trading and escapes from sea thieves off the China coasts. She was so fascinated by his tales that she stole away every day to meet him. The girl was Emmaline Trask Lowell, the fourteen year old daughter of Dr. Butler Lowell, once of Boston, but then of more liberal-minded San Francisco.

The Lowells were a very respectable family in Massachusetts. Young Doctor Butler Lowell had relatives enough to keep any young doctor comfortably occupied, —he was a cousin, though twice removed, of James Russell Lowell—but when he began to preach that "consumption was catching" and people with the dry cough should be put off by themselves, all the sisters and the cousins and the aunts turned against him. I guess there were too many in Massachusetts in that day rather proud of their dry cough as an added subject of conversation!

When the neighbors turn against a doctor there is only one thing for the doctor to do, and Dr. Butler Lowell did it. His move landed him in San Francisco.

Although Dr. Lowell had radical medical ideas his other notions were quite in accord with his family tradition. Which perhaps was the reason that Emmaline Lowell didn't tell her parents of the deckhand she had fallen in love with. Instead she eloped with her sailor to Niles, California. They kept their marriage a secret and a month later my father sailed for Samoa to be gone for a year. When he returned he found a baby son—my oldest brother.

My mother hated the sea. It took my father away from her sometimes for months, sometimes for two or three years. She never went with him, for the babies came along too fast—I was the eleventh!

Over a period of years Father worked himself up until he was the ranking captain of the Alaska Packers fleet of salmon ships. During the months his ship was frozen in, in Alaska, he learned the North like a book. He made charts of the wilds around Nome for the government. He prospected for gold; he went whaling for oil, and sealing for rich furs. He traded with the Eskimos, giving them tools, lumber and firearms in exchange for rare, carved ivory tusks of walrus, and polar bear skins.

I have always thought of Father as the swordfish of the ship. I began thinking of him that way the day I saw a swordfish and a whale in deadly combat.

Because of its size and the pictures they have seen of small boats being smashed by one sweep of its tail, most people naturally think of the whale as king of the ocean, but that impression is wrong. The swordfish is the boss. Both the whale and the shark are too slow and too clumsy to whip the real ruler of the sea. The swordfish doesn't grow beyond fifteen feet, but it fights because it likes to fight, and on occasion has driven its weapon ten inches through the copper and oak side of a ship.

We were in the trade winds about ten degrees north of the Equator one hot afternoon when, close to the ship and entirely without warning, a sperm whale leaped frantically clear and while in the air smacked down at the water savagely with its tail. The yell of the man at the wheel and the noise of that resounding slap brought all hands to the rail.

"Swordfish," said Father. "Nothing else ever made a whale jump out of the water."

Three times that whale jumped and what a thrashing about there was! The battle was ahead of us and a little to one side but neither fighter paid the slightest attention to the ship. The swordfish would come up from under to thrust at the tender underside of the whale. Then the whale would leap and come down lashing with its huge tail with terrific force to kill its attacker, but always in vain. In a few minutes the commotion quieted, the water was bloody. There was no whale in sight.

Father wasn't a large man, and every once in so often some whale of a sailor, deceived by his size, would undertake to defy him with force. Then followed the battle and Father always emerged the swordfish of the ship. Every time he won a battle his crew seemed prouder of him and he became kinder than before.

Just because I was the only girl on board I was not accorded any privileges that sailors didn't get. I went without food as they did when we were on a long trip and the provisions ran short. I stood my trick at the wheel steering, pulled at the ropes when we tacked, manned the pumps when the ship sprang a leak, said "Yes sir" to my father and was taught to obey as a sailor obeys the master of a ship. Above all I was taught the code of the sea:— never to squeal on anyone, take punishment without a squawk and be ashamed to show fear.

I had no other children to play with, no other womanthing on board, so my playthings were sea birds, little toy ships, and a lifeboat which was made fast to the deck and was seldom used. I would get in that lifeboat and pretend to row. I measured my strokes and counted a thousand strokes to the mile. In my lifeboat, strapped to the deck, I used to row away on long picnic trips by myself to places where I would find children to play with; children like I had seen playing around the docks in port. And what games we had! The games played with those imaginary children always involved something to eat.

You see, on a sailing ship bound on a voyage of one hundred and twenty days, the food is rationed so many ounces per person per day. Because I was little my rations rated one-half of a grown sailor's share. That was probably an excellent thing for my health but there was never a day when I couldn't have eaten four times as much—so food and playmates were my dreams of unattainable bliss. At my picnics we would set tables with piles of wonderful foods and I would eat all the things I wanted to. The only food I knew about was rough ship food, such as lentils, rice, salt beef in brine, dried fish and dried fruits. The sailors told me about delicious "vittles" that people on land had for every meal—fresh juicy apples and cakes and chickens stuffed with raisins and lots of sugar and real milk. Of course I thought the sailors just made up those things, so I pretended I really had them on my dream voyages. The children—and there were always thousands of them—would play with me. I had long conversations with them about pretty dresses and mothers and living in one house for a long time and waking up in the same place every day. I had these conversations out loud, but no one ever paid any attention to me because the crew and Father were too busy all the time to notice what I did. When my games were over I pretended the children were sorry to have me leave and I would promise to row back the next day and play with them again. But no matter where I went, or how far, I had to count my strokes carefully, because if I made a mistake, how could I ever get back to the ship? When my picnic was finished I'd climb back in the lifeboat and begin carefully counting my strokes for the return voyage until I had reached the proper number and knew it was safe to disembark from my stationary lifeboat to the deck of our schooner, once more just a sea captain's daughter.

Our trips usually took from eighty to one hundred and twenty days at sea without sighting land. Through storms, calms, waterless days—when our water casks ran dry—scurvy, and head winds, we travelled from port to port. If I ever felt fear I knew better than to express it. My father and the sailors had taught me a faith that made me hold on, no matter what happened. They believed there was God in the sunsets, in the storms, in the whiteness of an albatross's wing, and in the winds that blew our ship along.

Life at sea did not seem any mystery. An old sailor taught me that thunder was the growling curse of a dead sea captain who had lost his course; the blinding flashes of lightning were the combined sparkles of bar-maids' eyes luring seamen to a pleasant harbor; the groaning, creaking noises in the rigging and the hull of the ship which seemed so much louder at night were the tired squawkings of our schooner, her complaints at carrying such heavy cargoes. That was what I believed, but sometimes I knew that those noises were really seams that had opened under the stress of the pounding sea; that water was leaking into the hold as fast as the crew could pump it out—and the straining noises in the rigging told of weather-rotting blocks which might carry away at any minute. Every night before I turned in to my bunk I realized I might be going to sleep for the last time. There are so many dangers besetting a sailing ship on the deep seas that every sailorman knows the end may come at any moment. Yet in spite of that ghost which stalked the decks at night, I would fall asleep, unafraid.

Our sailors were the huskiest men Father could assemble—Swedes, Norwegians, Germans, Irishmen and Poles. What they lacked in brains they more than made up for in brawn. Natural-born rovers, they were content as long as we sailed, but when we hit port they floundered hopelessly in waterfront saloons, or in the islands where they went ashore, and the native girls, thrilled by their physiques and white skins, gave themselves freely. The native girls were fascinated by the white-skinned men off ships that sailed to their islands from the "lands beyond the horizon" and the sailors were more than willing to be adored gods to the little bronze beauties who caressed them and covered them with flowers. The fact that some day the question of sex would be an issue for me to face never occurred to me, for I had my whole world of people catalogued from my one-sided perspective on sailors. Mates were usually married to some faithful woman in the Old Country—Sweden; captains in my opinion, never drank or made love to women because they loved some woman in the States as my father loved my mother. Cabin-boys represented to me pimply youths just out of high school who ran away to sea for adventure and didn't find it, or dreamy boys who were too lazy to work ashore.

Cooks, because we had Japanese cooks, were heavenly people who would give me extra food.

As an antidote for unsavory influences such as perfume which I smelled on the cook and dreams of living in cities, Father made me take a salt water bath in a canvas tank on deck every day. Only when it rained did I get a fresh water bath.

There was no seaman's work that my father or the sailors didn't teach me. I learned arithmetic by adding up tide tables in navigation books. Before I was twelve I could take a "sight of the sun" and figure out our position on the chart. I learned to read "intelligent" things, as I termed them, from an old, battered set of the encyclopedia. We had a complete set except for the volumes from "N" to "S". As a result I had read everything in those encyclopedias except the subjects contained in the missing volumes.

Our ship's library, supplied by those well-meaning societies ashore that feel seamen need fine literature to uplift them, consisted of such books as "The Care and Feeding of Pedigree Dogs," "Modern Science of Surgery," "Engineering," Hymn books, Cæsar's Conquest (in Latin) and other such works guaranteed to inspire the minds of sailors to loftier ideals than the fleshpots. In desperation for something to read at sea the sailors would borrow the books, read them from cover to cover and return them to the library feeling rich in the priceless knowledge they imparted. Even I read them all and Father highly approved because he said they wouldn't fill my head full of silly notions. Once a sailor fell so low as to bring a sixpenny paper-covered novel on board entitled "Mad Love." The sailors all read it and I managed to get it by standing its owner's tricks at the wheel for two whole days. If it wasn't elevating, at least "Mad Love" appealed to me more than the "Care and Feeding of Pedigree Dogs." Some day, when I'm rich, I'm going to supply all the sailing ships in the world with real story books to avenge those years of barren reading which were foisted upon us by the uplift societies!

One of the chief accomplishments of our sailors was their spitting. They chewed tobacco and spat the juice freely. They could spit at a crack and hit it without a miss, and one sublimely endowed sailor could spit a curve to windward without mishap! I tried chewing tobacco, but the first time I chawed a hunk Father told me to swallow the juice if I wanted to be a good spitter. Obediently I swallowed a whole mouth full of bitter tobacco juice. The result was as expected. After that lesson I chawed dried prunes which made grand spit. After long weeks of practice I could not only spit at a crack but I could hit it, and it is on record that I spit two curves on a windy day, which gave me a high rating as an able bodied seaman!

When that woman was disapproving of me to John Henry because I lived on a ship, a man-raised child, I wondered if she could even spit straight herself, and if she couldn't, what did she know about our sea anyhow?

2

In which an alarm clock and some dried apricots are exchanged with natives for a nurse for me. The ship becomes my cradle

MY life at sea started when I was eleven months old. Father had brought me down to the schooner, a tiny bundle wrapped in a blanket. I was so small I would have been lost in his bunk, so Father had Stitches—the sailmaker—make a diminutive hammock of canvas. This hammock was swung from bolts, one sunk in the wall above the middle of Father's bunk and the other into the stanchion at the foot of the bunk on the outside. The rolling of the ship rocked the hammock more steadily than the most indulgent mother.

From the time he made my baby hammock, Stitches devoted his life to me. For fourteen years he thought of me first, then of the ship, last of himself, and in the final tragedy of our ship, he died to save me. I loved him and pestered him and abused his love as only a child can, but I'll never forget him.

I first recall Stitches as being the only man in the world

older than Father. In reality he must have been close to sixty when I was brought on board. His life was one of the romantic tragedies of the sea, for when he came to sign on the Ship's Articles he said "I'm a kind of Johnny-All-Sorts, Skipper. I've been all the way up and down the ladder from cabin-boy to Captain and back to sail-maker. My name's my own business, and I'll sign on in my own way, if you want me."

"Sign any way you damn please," answered Father, who knew a sailor when he saw one.

So the old sailor signed the Articles just "Stitches" and that's the way he was known for more than fifteen years on our ship. In appearance there was no sailor like Stitches. Years of bending over his work as sailmaker had brought his head forward and his stomach protruding full speed ahead. He waddled a little when he walked, and always sat tailor fashion with his legs crossed so that he gave the impression of a mild, wise old turtle upright on his tail. Every man on the ship came to Stitches with his troubles because they all knew that he had forgotten more about the sea than most men ever learn, and he had had so many troubles of his own that he understood.

Stitches must have been born lacking the iron in his soul to make him set his course and hold it. Rather he had chosen to ride before the storms of life, but as a compensation for his successive failures, he had developed his own peculiar philosophy of content that made the crew love him.

Why didn't Stitches give up the sea? He couldn't. The sea was in his blood and he would rather stay on a ship in any capacity than live ashore in comfort.

"I'll drop my final anchor with the wind howling in my ears above and the swish of bilge water below me," he declared, "and that way I'll go content." And when the time came, I'm sure he went content.

I had inherited my father's lusty lungs, and my crying did not help my popularity with the men trying to sleep on their watch below. The cabin-boy had to heat sea water in a saucepan over an oil lamp for my daily bath which Father gave me. My bathtub was an empty codfish keg, and how I yelled whenever I faced it. The mate usually turned in at nine in the morning and at that time I was always squalling my loudest. He made a remark which cost him his berth when it was repeated to my father.

"Damned if I ever thought I'd live to see the day when a deep water schooner would be made into a howling nursery."

Friends of my father along the waterfront in Frisco thought he was crazy to take a baby to sea. We were bound for Chile and thence to Australia. Father's friends reminded him that the trip was a hard one on account of sudden storms and freak weather off the west coast of South America.

"If I can handle a bunch of squareheads and a scow of a ship in a typhoon, a baby will be easy," was Father's answer to their warnings. With characteristic, clear vision he knew his course, and he determined to keep a strong hand on the helm of my life.

That trip, which was my first one, brought all the predicted complications. The patent foods which Father had provided to feed me did not agree with me. I lost weight and became so puny that Father had about given up hope that I would survive until we reached Sydney. There was only one thing for him to do and that was get some kind of food that would nourish me. We would not be in Australia for fifty or sixty days, so he turned in at Norfolk Island to see if he could buy something there to feed me.

"I tried to get a native woman with a small child to come on board and feed you from her breasts," Father told me years afterwards, "but she was afraid to venture beyond the horizon on a white-winged ship."

Not to be defeated in his mission, Father sent Stitches in one direction on the island and he went another, seeking some way of solving the feeding problem. Many search islands for treasure, but Father's exploring was for something more rare on a South Sea island—food for a sick baby. Native children are fed on yarrow roots and raw fish washed down their little throats with coconut milk, but white children can digest no such diet.

After combing the island all day Father returned to the ship, discouraged. He had begun to think finer things of the land than he had when he had taken me from my home to raise on the sea.

At about midnight Stitches came on board. With triumph in his face he rolled aft and asked permission to speak to Father.

"Cap'n, I found somethin' for the kid."

Father looked at Stitches' empty hands.

"Where in the hell is it?" he asked.

Stitches grinned.

"She's up in the fo'c's'le now. Come on and sign her on!" and he waddled out of the cabin followed by Father. Father thought "her" was some native woman that Stitches had coerced into coming on board. Stitches led the way under the fo'c's'le head and pointed to his prize.

"Cap'n, I had a helluva time gettin' that one, but I woulda got her if I had to kill all that tribe with me own fists."

Father looked through the shadows under the fore-peak and saw a terrified milch goat. The beast was balancing dizzily on her legs among the anchor chains.

"How'd you get it?" Father asked.

"Well, as I said, Cap'n, them natives wasn't gonna let me have her, and I figured I'd forfeit my sea boots if I'd let 'em out-talk me with that baby aft wastin' away, so I trades 'em an old alarm clock and a handful of dried apricots for this here dairy."

It was the best trade Stitches ever made. Father was so grateful for the goat that he appointed Stitches my nurse and guardian under him with the special privilege of talking back to Father on any matter concerning me without getting his block knocked off. His lesser reward was free tobacco so long as he stayed on the ship. For fourteen years to the day he died for me Stitches exercised all his special rights and privileges to the full. I grew to love him as a second father and I knew I was the mainspring of his life; knowing that, of course I took advantage of him every time I could.

The sailors named the goat "Wet Nurse" and to Wet Nurse and her generous supply of milk I owe my life today. In exchange for her milk Wet Nurse was fed oatmeal and coconuts.

After we put out to sea from Norfolk Island, Wet Nurse got seasick. Father knew that seasickness, like fright, will wear off if you don't pay any attention to it, so he bided his time. He was rewarded when Wet Nurse got her sea legs and gave milk freely. Stitches always said I had an appetite like a goat's because I could digest anything—so perhaps I inherited my iron stomach from Wet Nurse. For weeks I thrived on her milk, but it wasn't to be for long. Wet Nurse was not exactly ship broke in her personal habits. She needed a valet with a broom and pan if ship's orderliness was to be preserved. The crew took shifts of cleaning the decks where Wet Nurse took her exercise, with the result that she was not popular with the men forward! Wet Nurse got lonesome for her island home, and perhaps for her goat husband. She seemed to choose the hours when the sailors were sleeping to maaa her call. The sound of a she-goat calling her mate is not very beautiful, and it took all of Stitches' strength to fight off the sailors when they wanted to make Wet Nurse walk the plank! Father treated her as if she were a cabin passenger, and it would have been tough on any sailor who harmed her.

One day, when I was about two years old, our ship was caught in a white squall off Lord Howe Island. A white squall is a sudden wind storm that rises without warning on the barometer and its velocity is so great that it will sweep the sea with huge waves ten minutes after it starts. Wet Nurse was standing by the galley door looking wistfully at the cook in the hope of getting an occasional scrap or two from his pans, when the squall hit the ship.

Whipped by the wind the vessel listed far over to leeward and great seas washed over the decks. I was tied in my hammock below, for Father had called all hands on deck. The crew was reefing down the topsails and battening down the hatches. Father stood at the helm steering the ship out of the belly of the swells to keep the seas from swamping us. Everyone forgot Wet Nurse. A giant green wave came over the fo'c's'le head, washed over the galley, put out the cook's stove and drove Wet Nurse against the bulwarks. With a shudder the vessel hove to the windward side and another sea smacked her deck with such force that it lifted the fore hatch from its cleats and sent it swirling to the lee bulwarks pinning Wet Nurse beneath its wreckage.

She lay crippled and terrified and nearly drowned under the debris until the storm subsided. The mate and Stitches found her, and lifting her gently, as if she were a person, from beneath the hatch, they carried her up to the poop deck to my father. She had broken both her legs and several ribs were smashed in. Father, who has always had a gentle hand with animals, carefully set her legs in splints and bound her ribs with bandages made from small pieces of canvas. Then he lay Wet Nurse in his bunk beneath my hammock. In spite of everything he could do for her, Wet Nurse died that night. She was given a regular ship's funeral. The ship hove to for five minutes, as her body, sewn in sailcloth and weighted with a piece of chain, was committed to the deep.

And the next day I went on regular sailor's diet.

3

"A ship is called a 'she' because her riggin' costs more than her hull."
—*Stitches.*

FATHER had devised and carried out the scheme for nourishing a baby at sea, but another and more difficult problem for any man is clothing womenfolks.

When I was two years old I could walk and say "goddamned wind." That was my first sentence, which I picked up from the mate. I had outgrown my baby dresses—so something had to be done about it. On deep water vessels the crew, as well as the mates and captain, usually wear coarse dungarees and heavy woolens in cold weather, white cotton undershirts and short cotton trousers in the tropics. Shoes are worn only in port as it is too dangerous, as well as too expensive, for sailormen to walk around the slippery decks in leather soles.

When I began to walk by holding on to the rail of the poop deck we were off Easter Island, getting a load of guano, which is bird manure used for fertilizing purposes. It would be months before we hailed the main-

land, so again Father was ingenious in solving a difficulty. I had to have something to wear! Father turned
the fo'c's'le into a sewing room. His seamstresses were
Lars Erickson—a Dane, Scotty—an old Scottish sailor
who had only one snag tooth in his mouth and that brown
from tobacco stain, and the trusty Stitches.

These men were commissioned to make my wardrobe.
They cut a small pair of pants from Stitches' well worn
dungarees and made little suspenders on them. The
button-holes were works of art embroidered with infinite
pains by Stitches. While they were engrossed in their
sewing a Hungarian sailor who was a bit of a bully, by
name "Gooney" Bulgar, leaned out of his bunk and remarked:

"You ladies of the sewing circle will now adjourn an'
tea will be served in the Cap'n's parlor," with which he
waved an effeminate, coy hand in the shellbacks' faces.

It was never definitely settled which of them landed
on him first. Bulgar claimed that Stitches had scratched
him with his needle and none would bear witness that
Scotty and Erickson hadn't used a steel marlinspike on
him. At any rate he resembled a piece of raw hamburger
steak when they brought his limp body aft to my father
to be revived. If there is one thing prevalent on shipboard it is he-men, and any suggestion that impugns their
virility has to be settled with belaying pins to the finish.
Whatever really happened, the event is recorded in the
Log Book as follows:

"This day at sea, the 27th of September, Able-Bodied Seaman Gustav Bulgar fell, in the course of duty, off the
fo'c's'le head on to the main deck and was badly injured.

Treated by Captain. Given dose of salts and wounds painted with Friar's Balsam. Captain found it advisable to fine seaman Five Dollars for carelessness."

After that slight interruption to their sewing, the three men resumed, and turned out a complete wardrobe for me. Scotty had an old pair of rubber sea boots that were worn out at the bottoms so he cut off the tops, and turned out a pair of tiny rubber sea boots for me. With the remaining scraps he fashioned a sou'wester oilskin hat for me. He was at a loss for something to line it with, as the only available material on the ship was cast off clothing. A sailor never does anything by halves, and unless that sou'wester was lined, it was not complete in his estimation. As he was taking a mental inventory of the material he could lay hands on in the fo'c's'le, "Pimples," the cabin-boy, came in. It was his first trip at sea. He had come to get experiences so he could be a famous writer of sea stories like Jack London. He was still so green in the ways of the sea that he wore shoes and socks. Pimples had won his cognomen by his complexion which was caused half by adolescence and half by the food which fell to his lot after the crew and captain had eaten the best of it. It was unfortunate for Pimples that he intruded into the fo'c's'le at that moment, for Scotty saw his shoes and socks.

"Come here, Barnacles," he cooed to the cabin-boy. "Come closer so I can see how big your muscles are getting now you are at sea."

Pimples came over to him eagerly, happy to be recognized as an equal by a regular sailor. When he was close enough, Scotty tripped him, and sat on his stomach. While Pimples squirmed, Scotty took off his shoes and socks and, holding a brown woolen sock up for the others to see, he shouted:

"Here's the lining for the sou'wester," and then he booted the luckless cabin-boy out of the fo'c's'le.

When the little clothes were finished and the sock-lined oilskin cap proudly displayed, the sailors called in the Jap cook, Yamashita, to approve of their handiwork. The cook looked at them and then snorted with Oriental disapproval:

"Where nightgown for Missy? No damn sense sailor got." He went back to his galley and presently emerged with two bottles and three flour sacks. The bottles contained cake frosting coloring, red and green. He took some string and dipped it in the red and made red string, and then dipped some more string in the green. These colored strings he used to embroider intricate cross stitch designs on the neck and arms of the flour sack nightgown and dress. In spite of his many washings of the sacks to remove the printing on them, a dim memory of the words, "Pure as the drifted snow," remained on them forever.

I wore overalls all my life on board the ship. Father kept me dressed as a boy in fairness to the crew and for my protection. He did everything in his power to keep them and me from becoming conscious of my sex. When I was big enough to wear them Father bought me regular men's size overalls. They buttoned in front and I was very proud that even in my clothing I resembled the sailors.

The first time I wore a dress after I left the ship I didn't know how to walk in it. The skirt got tangled up in my legs and kept me from taking long sea strides. I had to wear underclothes with a dress and they seemed to stifle my body that was used to salt soaked overalls next to a bare skin. It was a tragic day for me when Father informed me that with a dress I had to wear shoes and stockings. The shoes hurt my feet and the cotton stockings itched—but more of the impediments of civilization later.

To go back to my babyhood— When a young lady is big enough to walk, able to say "goddamned wind" and to occupy the attention of three tailors, it is obviously time to begin thinking about her education. Father and Stitches consulted gravely.

"The fust thing she's gotter learn, Cap'n," argued Stitches, "is to keep from fallin' overboard."

"All right," agreed Father, "every time you catch her near the rail, paddle her bottom."

Stitches nodded in partial approval.

"That's all right, too, Cap'n, but kids is natcha'lly ornery and their sterns gits calloused, awful fast."

Father saw the point.

"We'll tie her up," he said.

So they put me at the end of a fifteen foot rope tied to the wheelbox on the poop deck. That was fine for a few days until in a sudden blow I got the rope around the steersman's feet, with the result that my head and his stern nearly broke the deck and the ship got off her course.

Stitches and Father again went into conference.

"In one week she's slipped her hawser twice and tripped up the steersman. We gotter try somethin' else, Cap'n," urged Stitches. Father thought it over.

"Sooner or later she's pretty sure to go overboard any-how, so you'd better teach her to swim."

"That's a fine idea, Cap'n," replied Stitches, "only I don't know how to swim myself." Which is one of the queer things about the sea: more than half of the sailors can't swim.

"You fix a tank. I'll teach her," decided Father.

Just aft the mizzen mast, Stitches rigged up a canvas tank about four feet square and equally deep. This was collapsible, so that when it was empty it could be folded up and put in the cabin out of the way of the storms. It was a sailor's job to fill it with sea water every morning. This he did by throwing overboard a canvas bucket in which he baled up a hundred gallons of water to fill it. When it was full he reported the fact to my father. Then Father would go to my hammock, get me and carry me down to the tank. I was a wiggling, squirming, protest-ing bundle of muscular little girl, as husky as a seal, and full of objections to the idea of being pulled out of a comfortable warm hammock and plunged naked into a cold sea dip.

The routine was always the same. Before he plunged me into the tank he would roll me on the deck. Then he made me turn somersaults, and box with him. My share of the boxing might be described as down again, up again. As soon as I could get to my feet he would tum-ble me over with his pawlike hand, and keep that up for about ten minutes. If I cried or protested at all against that rough treatment I got a sound slap on my bottom to "knock that nonsense out of you." Then came the great moment when, warm and glowing, I was plopped into cold sea water to strike out blindly, and in vain. Holding his hand under my back, Father told me to throw out my stomach and bend my head back to balance. I couldn't understand how that would help me float because when I put my head back I got my mouth and ears and eyes full of salt water. Then he explained it in words to penetrate my infant comprehension.

"Throw your head back and puff your stomach up until YOU CAN SEE YOUR BELLY-BUTTON."

Then it became a game, and in my eagerness to see if I could puff my stomach up high enough for me to see that portion of my anatomy, I achieved the art of floating. While I was thus absorbed in watching myself perform, Father took his bracing hand from under my back and left me to my own resources. Once I had learned to float, swimming came easy and I soon outgrew the limitations of the four foot tank. I didn't think I had, but Father did. The next port we arrived in was Newcastle, Australia, and he chose that harbor to polish off my swimming ability.

When he looked for me to begin another lesson he found me playing with a tame gooney on the deck, perfectly contented. A gooney is a species of gull, dull grey in coloring, and a bit larger than the common seagull. Father had snagged him on a big hook baited with a piece of salt pork, pulled him aboard and clipped his wings so he could not fly away. When we first got him the gooney tried to bite, but by feeding him a few days he became tame, and quite a fascinating toy for me. We had named him "Salt Pork."

We were playing a game called "Grub" which Stitches had invented for us. "Grub" was a unique game in that it gave me my first philosophy of doing things for myself and increased my propelling powers immensely. The rules for "Grub" were simple. A line was drawn on the poop deck with chalk behind which Salt Pork and I lined up. The goal was a piece of bread on the rail aft by the wheel. At a given signal from Stitches he let go of Salt Pork and off we both went across the deck after the grub; me, a hungry kid and Salt Pork, a ravenous sea bird. I crawled on all fours after it and the gooney ran with webbed feet. If I got there first I ate the bread on the spot as fast as I could cram it down my gullet or Salt Pork would have grabbed it right out of my hand. If Salt Pork got it first I couldn't get it away from him because he'd swallow it whole without even chewing it.

"Say, Stitches," called Father from the gangway, "let's give Joan a lesson in keeping her mouth shut!" He undressed me and took me to the fo'c's'le head. Two of the crew were cooling off with a nice swim under the shadow of the bowsprit. He called to them to keep an eye on me and without further warning he threw me fifteen feet into the water below. I thought I had sunk to the bottom of the world and would never come up. When I finally did I was so frightened that I started to yell and was rewarded with a mouthful of salt water. There was nothing to hang on to, so I had to swim. My father and Stitches on the jib-boom above laughed at my struggle. Of course there was no danger for me as the two sailors could have pulled me out in an instant. It seems useless to add that I learned to swim in deep water very rapidly.

Father, evidently satisfied that Lesson Number One in practical nautical knowledge was a success, remarked to Stitches:

"See how quick she shut her mouth when she hollered

about nothing! If every woman could learn to keep her mouth shut at the age of two they'd be better off."

Every day after that, during the weeks we were in Newcastle, I was thrown overboard. I came to love it and soon was a strong swimmer with an instinct for action instead of noise!

4

In which I learn that young ladies must not take baths in gentlemen's drinking water

FROM the time I was two years old until about my sixth birthday nothing startling impressed itself on my baby mind. Ours was just the usual routine of a trading schooner: Seattle to Sydney with lumber and from Sydney it was "bound to the South Sea Islands for copra," loaded with red calico, cheap knives, soap, tinfoil, anything shiny to catch the eyes and thrill the hearts of the natives.

We cruised from island to island picking up half a ton of copra here, a quarter ton there until we had filled the hold, and for a deck load we got generally about five hundred bundles of sandalwood. Of course we took lots of smaller stuff, but copra and sandalwood were our staples from the islands.

Copra—the word itself is common to sea traders, but to landlubbers it is a strange expression found in stories of the South Seas.

Copra is the meat of coconuts dried in the sun. The natives break open the nuts and lay them out on woven mats to rot. The rotting process in the tropic heat brings out the oils and acid of the coconut. It takes about three months of drying process to make the copra rotten enough to be ready for market. The natives load it in bales of reeds and carry it off the island in canoes to waiting ships.

In appearance copra is dark brown and fibrous. No copra is first class until it is so putrid that vermin infest it. The stench of it is almost unbearable. In its ripe stage copra is highly explosive. During the war many uses were found for the stuff. The waste of its matter was used for ammunition, the oils to preserve foods for the soldiers, and the acids were invaluable in surgery.

One of the most common uses of copra is in the manufacture of linoleum and some forms of paper. I often wonder when people are walking on the linoleum in their homes if they realize that the substance of it came from the savage islands of the South Seas.

In trading between the islands, Australia and the States in my early years our greatest rival and bug-bear was the barkentine, *Mary Winklemund,* a three-master under the command of Captain Swanson. A barkentine by reason of its rig, square yards on the fore mast, is naturally faster than a schooner and the *Mary Winklemund* for years won every race with the *Minnie A. Caine,* whether it was from Hawaii to New Zealand or from Samoà to Seattle. My father and Captain Swanson were rivals, both in shouting the praise of their ships and in pride of their navigation, but Swanson had the edge. He would beat us by a few hours, by a few days, and on occasion by two months. Father always blamed the bad winds and incompetent sailors, and said that Swanson was afraid to carry as big a load as we for fear of sinking. But in spite of his alibis, the fact remained that in every nautical endeavor Swanson made us look like a leaking lifeboat in a hurricane.

Naturally to a man of Father's combative temperament being beaten was bad enough, but Captain Swanson, not content with winning, never let a chance go by to rub in the victory with heavy-handed sea humor. As a result Father, I believe, would have run his ship on the rocks or jumped overboard himself, if thereby he could have scored on that "goddamned, squareheaded Sea Hog," as he always delicately described his rival. How Father did even up the score stuck in my mind because it was combined with the memory of my first attempt at the age of six to get rich quick.

We were anchored in Double Bay, Sydney, my sixth winter, and Swanson sent word to Father to come aboard the *Mary Winklemund* for dinner. Father sent back word that he would accept free grub even on the *Winklemund*. I was delighted, for I welcomed any opportunity to get off our own vessel. As we were leaving in a small boat to skull over to the *Winklemund* Father turned to me and said:

"Swanson is trying to show off to me what good grub they serve on his packet. I'll paddle you if you dare eat like you enjoy it."

When we boarded the *Mary Winklemund* by means of a Jacob's ladder thrown over the side, Captain Swanson met us. He showed us around his ship which was newly painted white from stem to stern. He pointed out the ship's fine points, not forgetting to tell just where and how much she excelled ours. Father was getting madder and madder all the time and I was afraid he would blow up and go back without waiting for dinner.

"And just to show you how much better and cheaper I manage my ship," concluded Captain Swanson, "look at this." He reached into a barrel and brought out a small piece of something that looked like dirty marshmallow.

"See that, Captain?" he boasted. "Well, I had a whole barrel of it. Used it to oil down the masts this trip, saved me buying oil. Maybe if you was to oil down the sticks on your ship you could sail faster."

Father took the substance from his hand, and smelled it, and looked up. I was surprised to see all the mad had gone out of his face.

"Got any more of this?" he asked, and there was a twinkle in his eye.

"Naw, I ain't got no more. When we struck hot weather it stunk to high heaven so I throwed it over the side."

"How much have you got left?"

"Just about a bucketful in this barrel," he answered. "And I told the ship's chandler he could have it. He asked me for it."

"The hell you say," observed my father, and I thought I saw him smile. "You're a smart old barnacle, aren't you, Swanson?" Swanson puffed in pride, and led the way to the dining saloon. There before us was a meal intended to impress Father with its luxuriousness. I looked at it glumly, remembering Father's words, "I'll paddle you if you eat like you enjoy it." How could anybody eat all that food and not show enjoyment? He must have seen what was in my mind for he slapped me on the shoulder, exclaiming: "Forget it, Joan. Eat all you can and enjoy every bit of it. I'm going to."

I had my mouth full before they were in their chairs, but, once squared away, I never saw Father eat so much or enjoy it so heartily. When he finished he pushed back his chair, looked at Swanson and burst out laughing.

"What's so funny?" asked Swanson uncomfortably.

"Nothing, you big squarehead, but do you know what that grease is you threw overboard?"

"Naw. I found it floating off the Gilbert Islands. Saw some sea birds picking at it, so I put off a boat and investigated. Looked like good grease so I hauled a couple of barrels aboard and used it like I told you to grease down the masts."

"They're fine sticks, Swanson," grinned Father. "They ought to be, greased down with a hundred thousand dollars worth of ambergris."

Swanson gulped and turned pale. His eyes were almost popping out of his head.

"Huh? Ambergris?" he gasped.

"Yes, ambergris!" shouted Father. "Worth thirty-two dollars an ounce. And you threw a barrel of it overboard. You threw away a fortune, you goddamned, ignorant, stingy squarehead." And Father lay back in his chair and roared with laughter.

Swanson was livid now. "You think you're smart, don't you?" he yelled. "Only don't forget this—there was twice as much stuff there as I took. I know where it is and I'll go back and get it."

"Good luck," laughed Father, "if you can find it again you're entitled to it."

"I'll find it," were the grim parting words of the squarehead Captain.

Going back in the small boat to our ship I asked Father what ambergris was.

"Whale vomit," he answered.

I couldn't see what was so funny about Swanson throwing away whale vomit so I persisted in questioning further.

"What's it good for?"

"Joan, ambergris is worth thirty-two dollars an ounce. He threw away about sixty thousand dollars worth just through ignorance."

"Well, what's the good of whale vomit? Why is it worth money?"

"Perfume companies use it as the base for rare perfume. And I wish to Christ I could find some."

"Why don't you try and find what Captain Swanson left?"

"Because anybody but an old fool like Swanson would know that sea birds eat ambergris. What he left is gone long ago. I only hope he does hunt it. It will keep him off the trade route for six months."

And that is exactly what happened. Captain Swanson spent six months looking for his ambergris and found nothing. But Father told the story in every port and nowhere Swanson went did seafolk allow him to forget it.

I couldn't forget ambergris either. If Swanson could find it why couldn't we? There must be some way of locating it.

But the more I thought the more discouraged I became. A few barrelsful of ambergris in a whole ocean—

not much chance of finding that. Then like a flash the idea came to me. It was so simple I wondered why Stitches or Father or some other sea captain had not thought of it. All I had to do was just to make the whales in the ocean sick at their stomach and they would belch forth ambergris enough to fill our ship. And that much I figured would be worth millions and millions and Father would never have to worry about bad trading seasons or port charges any more. We put to sea in a week and were headed for the Union Group of islands about twenty-eight degrees latitude South, one hundred and sixty-seven degrees longitude West. There ought to be some whales around there. I thought if I poisoned the water in the sea all the whales would be sick. The only drawback to my scheme was that I didn't have any poison, so I made some of my own.

I begged an empty codfish keg from the cook and poured some cold split pea soup in it. I hated split pea soup so I was sure that was poison. Then I emptied the spittoon from the wheel which was full of tobacco juice and spit into the soup. To this I added tar and some dead rats. The finishing touch was some dead cockroaches. I caught them and mashed them up in the mixture, and then, positive that I had concocted a potion to ruin all the whales, I waited for nightfall.

About ten o'clock that night I slipped to the lee rail and dumped my poison into the sea, and waited. For hours, I waited, straining my eyes against the darkness, searching the water for some signs of ambergris to float. At four bells I turned in, and spent the rest of my night at my porthole looking for a promise of a seasick whale, but of course there was none. My scheme to poison the entire ocean failed, and when the cook found that I had wasted a pot full of good pea soup, I got a licking for my effort. To this day the only consolation I have for my failure is that when I detect rare perfume on beautiful ladies, I speculate with pleasure as to what they would think if they knew the base of their scent was whale vomit!

As long as I was a baby the sailors thought me a grand toy to play with and make a fuss over but when I grew old enough to become a bother their kindly attitude was frequently subject to change.

Of course it is the common belief that when a captain has a girl aboard ship the sailors slay each other to get the captain's beautiful daughter—that her very presence on shipboard uplifts them and inspires them to lofty ideals.

That might be the case in novels, but in real life it is far more practical! Never in all my experience did any sailor attempt any act of violence to gain my favor. Their acts of violence, at times, were directed against me instead.

It was on our next voyage after Father squared accounts with Captain Swanson that I saw my first real mutiny and felt what it was like to have an entire ship's crew against one. It all came about in the most natural way from being caught in the doldrums with a short water supply.

Our ship carried our fresh water supply in a tank under the fo'c's'le head and in two iron tanks lashed on the poop deck just aft of the spanker mast. These tanks contained in all about five thousand gallons of water, to be used by sixteen people over a period of from eighty to

one hundred and twenty days at sea. It was a precious
commodity and it was guarded zealously by the cook
whose job it was to portion it out daily, three cups to a
person. In the tropics the water became so hot and stag-
nant that "wigglers" came out in it. Wigglers are small
worms which hatch in the water. It is an old maritime
law that every "off-shore" vessel must carry a certain
amount of lime juice as a preventative against scurvy. A
drop of lime juice in a mug of water kills the wigglers
and thus enables the consumer to drink water without
live stock in it. To this day old English sailing ships are
referred to as "lime juicers," and that name came down
to them from the old custom.

We had been out eighty-three days from Mukelteo,
bound for Brisbane, Australia, with a million feet of lumber. The water supply ran very low, and the residue was
so alive with tiny wigglers and germs that it was like a
death warrant to drink it. The cook came aft and told
Father that a plague would come on the ship from that
water. The stench of it was terrible. Even the rats were
boldly searching the decks for something fresh. We were
in the doldrums, about eleven degrees south of the
Equator. The ship just wallowed in the glassy sea, and
seemed to crack and shrivel in the heat. There was no
shade anywhere. The sails hung limp and useless, like
unstarched linens. The bedbugs and roaches seemed to
multiply by the million.

"All hands on deck," ordered my father, and the mate
repeated his order to the men sleeping below. In a few
minutes the entire crew were on deck.

"There's no more water, men, until we hit a rain squall.
The glass is down and I look for a squall, so stand by

with kegs and catch all the rain you can if you want fresh water."

There was a mad hurry to get kegs to catch the rain. The men brought everything from salt pork barrels to empty tomato tins and placed them under the booms and scuppers. The cook and a sailor put a barrel under the drain on the main deck just below the poop deck to catch the water that washed down the poop.

No sailor tried to sleep any more. They sat huddled in the scuppers looking thirstily at the deceitful clouds that drifted by and disappeared to the horizon with their refreshing cargoes.

Night came, and still no sign of rain. Just at sunset, at about a quarter point off the starboard bow, appeared the end of a rainbow, dipping right into the sea and making an arch of vivid colors, which dissolved into the mist of a rain squall a mile away. It was aggravatingly near, and the men bent every inch of sail to hurry the ship into its midst to catch some of its rain, but just within a hundred yards of it, the little gust of wind died, and once more the sails hung limp and impotent.

That night for dinner we had a sticky mess of salt dried codfish. Its odour was so bad from the intense heat that the only way it could be swallowed was to smother it with mustard and hold your breath, to kill the smell.

"This damn stuff stinks," observed the mate, whereupon he proceeded to pick out the remnants of fish from his teeth with the prongs of his fork. I was just old enough to recognize the expression on my father's face as a sign of trouble.

"Yeh? Well any time you get disgruntled about the menu on this packet, just write me a letter and I'll file it in my correspondence." The mate's remark, however, spoiled his appetite and he shoved the dish of ill smelling fish at the cabin-boy.

"Chuck that overboard."

For my dinner I had boiled lentils, which only accentuated my thirst, as the salt fish had increased the men's.

At sea a very little thing will start a feeling of mutiny, and thirsty, dried-up men, scorched by heat and discouraged by no winds and bad food, are like dynamite to handle. They started to quarrel among themselves, viciously. Father anticipated trouble. Right after dinner he sent me to my bunk.

"And if you hear anything on deck, you stay below," he added and swung up to the poop deck. He searched the horizon for some sign of a storm to bring relief. If another day passed and no fresh water fell, there was no foretelling what uprising would occur. The sky was red, and the old legend, "Red sky at night, sailor's delight" gave no promise that the morning would bring water.

Father heard the men mumbling in the scuppers, for in some way they blamed him for their plight. Old Stitches, whose loyalty to father was like iron, came up on the poop deck beside him, and casually started to smoke his pipe. Beneath his nonchalance were grim, tight lips. He knew there was going to be trouble, and he wanted Father to know he was still swinging a belaying pin on his side.

I could feel something was going on that I didn't understand, and whenever I felt there was something being kept from me I just had to find out about it. So after I had been sent to bed, I sneaked back on deck and hid out of sight of Father. Nobody on the ship was asleep. I could hear the men stirring and grumbling for'ard.

Hour after hour passed, and in the deadman's watch, which was from twelve midnight until four, the men broke. Larsen, who had always been one of the best sailors, led the rest of the crew up on the poop deck, seething and snarling.

"What do you want?" roared my father.

"WATER!"

"Where in the hell will I get water for you?" Father asked, as he eyed the men who were closing in on him.

"WATER," came the accusing chorus again.

Stitches put down his pipe, and edged closer to Father.

"The barometer is low, we ought to run into a squall 'fore daybreak," explained Father.

"Yeh? Well we want water NOW, do you hear, and if you don't give us some, you and your goddamned ship will be sucking water in hell!" And with that two of the sailors jumped for him, and hit out with terrific blows, the blows of thirst-crazed men. Father hit back, and his punch was like a shot of steel. Stitches struck blindly with the belaying pin. Blood smeared the deck. I could hear a sickening, crunching sound of bones breaking. Slowly, one by one, the two of them backed the cowed men on to the main deck. I scuttled back to my berth and hid myself under my straw mattress.

Stitches came below and I heard him fumbling in the gun rack near my bunk.

"Nothin' like being watchful in nights like this," he said, and he came back on deck with two rifles. For the rest of the night the two of them stood off the men on the deck below.

Morning came early, for the sun rose at five-thirty. I was on deck early, too uncomfortable to stay below, and fretful from thirst. About six o'clock a black cloud which looked like a splotch of ink on the sky appeared on the horizon. A light breeze scurried it towards us. In ten minutes it was upon us, and rain fell in great cool sheets on the swollen decks and the parched lips of the men. They fought each other for places at the drains to grab the first water. They were like frenzied, caged animals suddenly loosed on raw meat as they opened their mouths to let the rain pour in.

I stood on the poop deck, under the spanker boom, and the water fell on me. It was so cool, so caressing, so life-giving! I couldn't soak enough of it in, it seemed, so I took off my overalls, and let it rain on my naked body. I was so absorbed in my fresh water bath that I was oblivious to the men standing on the main deck to catch the water that washed off the poop. I would do my bath up right! A real fresh water bath with soap!

Naked, and unconscious of the threats of the men who objected to my being in their way, I ran forward to the galley and asked the cook for some soap. He made soap from the grease drippings of the salt pork. To the grease he added lye and kept the conglomeration in a kerosene can under his bunk. I grabbed a handful of it, and began smearing it on me as I ran aft once more, and up to my place under the spanker boom. I was a mass of sticky bubbles, and the rain carried them, after they washed off me, down the drain into the waiting kegs of the crew. The soap suds ruined their water. Two of them leaped up on deck by me and were about to choke me when my father interfered. He grabbed me by my slippery body and put me behind him, while he ordered the men down on deck.

Then he turned to me.

"What the hell's the big idea?" he yelled, so enraged with me he was pale.

"It feels so goddamned good to get cool in the fresh rain," I answered. The humor of my remark didn't appeal to him. I could see I was going to get another licking, and my bare body was a good target for a rope's end!

"I'll teach you to spoil fresh water," he said, and he went forward. He returned with a handful of the soap!

"Now open your mouth. You're so anxious to be washed clean, just taste that," and he washed the inside of my mouth with the rotten soap.

And I've never wanted to be washed clean since then!

5

Perfume on the cook's feet and hair on my chest.—What of it?

As I grew up, strong and healthy, I had three very simple ambitions in life: to be able to hand, reef and steer; to spit as far as any Swede could; and to get as much food, if not more, than anyone else. On sailing ships the food is portioned out in what is called "whack;" that is, so many ounces of food per week is allotted to each person. There was no way of definitely estimating the exact number of days a trip would take, as we depended entirely on winds to blow us to our destination.

We carried no fancy foods—there wasn't room for anything except plain necessities in the storerooms. Lentils, rice, salt beef pickled in barrels of brine, dried codfish, powdered milk, dried prunes and apricots for desserts on holidays, and lime juice. The stores were stowed in an after-hold and were kept under lock and key. Only the Jap cook and my father had keys to that sanctum of grub and they guarded them relentlessly. The locked storeroom made life a bit difficult for me. I never seemed to get enough to eat. For instance, breakfast consisted of a big dish of cooked oats, dry bread and coffee. When the cabin-boy rang the breakfast bell it had the effect of a fire alarm and we all stampeded to the dining saloon. The first one that got to the table grabbed the bowl of mush and scraped off a big pile on his plate. I soon learned to grab the quickest. I developed in me the ability to take care of myself. Once a week, on Thursday, we had duff pudding. Duff day at sea was always an occasion. The cook prepared a sticky, glutinous mess of steamed suet and flour and put a few raisins in it. Plum duff it was called, but I always thought the cook put the pudding at the top mast and tossed plums at it, always missing, for I never could find any fruit in it. Weeks became important to me because of the plum duff pudding, and instead of saying of the future, "next week," I always calculated next duff day, or two duff days ago. Frequently the salt horse, as the pickled beef was nicknamed, stank so that I couldn't eat it, and neither could the sailors without drowning out the smell with mustard pickles, and holding their breath as they swallowed it. Sometimes by way of variety of menu, the bread took on the appearance of raisin bread, but the raisins were unfortunate cockroaches that had dived into the dough when the cook was kneading it. Little fresh meat additions like that never killed our appetites.

The final blow to my father's æsthetic sense came one day at lunch time. Father bit into a crust of bread and then his face became livid with anger.

"Slops!" he yelled at the cabin-boy. We had a new boy every trip. "What kind of so and so does the cook call this bread? It stinks of perfume like some barmaid."

"I don't know, sir. The cook just baked that bread fresh this morning," answered Slops. There was never any love lost between the cabin-boy and the cook and I think that Slops was enjoying the prospects that confronted his enemy.

I tasted the bread. It tasted of perfume, or rather of bay rum, the stuff the Jap cook always smelled of, but I couldn't figure out how it had got into the bread.

Father left the table and hurried forward to the galley, with me in his wake.

"Yamashita! Come out of your rat hole." The cook, trembling in fear, looked up from where he was sitting on the edge of the bunk.

"Yes sir?" he asked, as he continued washing his feet.

"Let me see the pan you mixed this bread in."

Yamashita looked up at Father in all innocence and replied, "This pan, Captain. This pan I wash my feet in!" Father let a snort of rage out and grabbed at the cook. He shook him within an inch of his life, and would have hit him if the cook had been anywhere near his size. I beat it aft to get out of the fight, for the cook was my friend.

Every time I got a chance to sneak forward to his galley I did so, and would sit on his lap listening to his stories of Japan. I would tolerate his tales, just so he would let me sit on him and smell his bay rum. The odor of it was exquisite to me, for everyone else on the ship smelled of rope and tobacco. I often measured a person's worth by the smell of him. One day an American consul's wife came aboard, and she smelled of some delicious powder. When I got a good sniff of it I said to her:

"You don't stink like men do, do you?" I intended it for a compliment, but the woman took umbrage and left in great haste, mumbling something about the uncouth persons that lived on ships!

No two days at sea were ever alike. Even in the monotonous trade winds, with the breeze so steady that the wheel could be lashed down and the ship would keep on her course alone, something would happen. It was on such a day as that that John McLean, an able-bodied seaman, won my heart. He was a huge, lumbering sailor with more muscle than brain, and was so crabby that the other sailors were afraid of him. He was always friendly with me in his rough sort of way because I would sit by the hour at his feet and admire him. On his chest, which was covered with hairs, he had a tattooed, full-rigged ship under sail that was one of my prize sights. If he was in a good humor he would undo his shirt and let me see that ship, then wiggle his chest so that the ship looked as if it were in a storm. Then he would bulge out his chest muscles and the ship looked as if it were under sail in a fair wind, or else he relaxed his chest and it looked becalmed in a lifeless sea.

"Gee, McLean," I exclaimed, "do you think I could ever have a ship on my chest?"

He moved his wad of tobacco to the other side of his cheek, looked at me scornfully and then condescended to answer:

"Naw, can't be tattooed like me unless you got hair on your chest."

That finished me, for my chest was as smooth as a piece of silk. But I wasn't to be outdone. I went to my father and asked him what made hair grow on people's chest. That question played right into his hand because he replied:

"Hair on your chest, Joan? Well, let me see. I warrant if you was to eat your pea soup every meal that would grow hair on your chest."

And I hated pea soup, but if it was necessary to cause a growth on my chest like McLean's, I would endure it. So for weeks I ate the pea soup with the secret consolation that some morning I would awake with a thick crop of hair on my chest. We arrived in Adelaide, South Australia, and still no hair on my chest. I was worried for fear I would probably never be able to grow any, so I went to McLean who was in the hold of the ship unloading copra.

"McLean," I confided, "I've looked every morning for nine weeks and there isn't any hairs on me yet—not even any fuzz. What shall I do?"

He grinned, one of his rare indulgences, and said:

"Hey, Skipper, is the Old Man aboard?"

"No, he isn't. He's up at the American Consul's office this morning."

McLean continued to grin for a moment, then said:

"All right, Skipper. We got an hour to knock off at noon, and I'll take you up to be tattooed."

"Really, McLean? You're not filling me with wind?" I could hardly believe my ears.

"Sure. I know the best tattooer this side of Tokio. He's just a quarter of a mile from here, back of the fish store and ship chandler's."

I was elated. I was to be like a real sailor, tattoo and everything! McLean had offered to take me and have it done because in his inarticulate way he liked me, and in his own mind he was being very generous to pay for me to be tattooed. It never occurred to a deep sea sailor like him that girls are not tattooed.

At noon time I was ready, waiting for him at the gangway. I had put on my sailor cap which was an old mate's cap elaborately embroidered with anchors and little ships and fish by the sailors. McLean kept his promise to meet me, and hand in hand we walked up the dock. My feet hardly touched the ground, I was so happy. We plotted what we would have put on me. I decided I wanted a naked lady in red tattooed on my forearm, a full-rigged ship on my breast and an American flag on the bottom of my foot so I could stick it out of the porthole and make it look as though I was waving a flag. If I was to be tattooed I was going to do it up right!

As we walked up the dock I saw Father standing by the warehouse talking to the boss stevedore. I was so exultant that I let my enthusiasm get the best of my discretion and I yelled at him:

"Ain't I swell? I'm going to be tattooed all over like a sailor."

Like a shot he wheeled around and said, "WHAT?"

"I said I'm going to have a naked lady tattooed on my arm near my elbow so I can move my arm and wiggle her stomach like she was dancing."

A murderous look came on his face. I turned around and saw McLean hotfooting it down the dock back to the ship! I followed him in haste, for Father grabbed me by the seat of my pants and the nape of my neck and propelled me along the dock at double speed.

"I can't leave you for five minutes but that you get into

some kind of deviltry, so now I'll teach you how to be-have."

He took me up on the poop deck and tied me to the wheel in full sight of the sailors. My heart was broken with disappointment, but no tears for mine. I stood there and swore all the words that I knew, and at that age my vocabulary included enough adjectives to keep me swear-ing two minutes without repeating a word.

As if it wasn't humiliation enough to be tied up like a bad puppy, the mate came aft and heard me swearing. I started all over again when he came near and looked at me. I could have murdered him for laughing at me. He listened to me going it and then scratched his head and said:

"I'll forfeit my grub if you can't cuss as good as if you had hair on your chest."

Oh, the music of his words! I pulled my jumper closer together so that he couldn't see if I had hairs or not, but having him think I did have hair on my chest was almost as good as really having it, so the day wasn't lost after all.

6

A dead fish and a squarehead's kiss

I WAS seven years old when I first met Fear, and what happened at the meeting and what followed did more to shape my character and life than anything I can remember. For I learned the important lesson that if I stuck to the code of the sea never to squeal, no matter what happened, but to fight my own battles in my own way—I could win against odds, provided I licked Fear.

It all came about through Stitches teaching me to fish. Of course careful old Stitches had too much sense to start me after deep sea fish, for they are so heavy and powerful that one might have yanked me overboard before help could reach me.

"You can practice gettin' little ones first, Skipper," he said, as he baited a line with a cockroach for me. "If you get a pull, take your line in easy."

I fished every day for weeks, and never got so much as a nibble. As I hadn't had any luck deep sea fishing, I tried casting my line in the harbor at Sydney. Father was ashore attending to bills of lading, and the crew were cleaning up the ship, painting, chipping paint and reeving on new canvas.

I felt a nibble; the line twitched, and I pulled with all my seven-year-old strength on it. On the hook was a flat fish about six inches long with huge bulging eyes. He wiggled and squirmed, but I got him in my fist and called to anyone who could hear to come and see my catch. Alex Svenson, a Norwegian sailor, who was holystoning the poop deck, came over to look at my fish.

"Ain't he a whopper?" I asked him, full of pride and enthusiasm. Svenson picked up the fish in his big paw and grunted a negative.

"This is a bloody bullfish. It ain't no good to eat," he said, and he ground the fish under his heel and laughed at my tears of disappointment.

No one ever fought my battles except myself, and this insult to my first catch was cause for war.

"That's my fish, you bloody squarehead," I shouted at him, as I grabbed my shining treasure and stuck it inside the bib of my overalls next to my skin.

"I'll kill you for making fun of my fish," and I kicked Svenson on the shins as hard as I could. But kicking a six foot Scandinavian on the shins with bare feet is not to be recommended. I only stubbed my toes and the more I kicked the more they hurt and the louder Svenson laughed. Ordinarily he was vile-tempered, but now my helpless rage seemed to please him.

"Say, you got a helluva lotta spirit, ain't you?" he grinned in my face.

"You killed my fish. I'll kill you, do you hear? You just wait!"

"Now be a nice little girl and don't get your temper up and I'll give you a big box of candy."

I was young enough for the prospect of candy to be a pacifier for any woe. My father never let me have any, and the rare occasions when the sailors sneaked it to me made me regard heaven as the place where you got all the candy you wanted.

Wiping away my tears with a fishy hand I forced a smile.

"I bet you ain't got any candy," I challenged him.

"Well, don't you squeal to Stitches or the Old Man, and I'll give you a whole box just for yourself."

I promised him I wouldn't betray him, and he went forward to get it. I twisted up my fish line in a neat coil while I waited for him. Presently I saw him coming aft with something concealed behind his back.

"Where is it?" I asked, a bit suspicious that he was only fooling me.

Svenson looked up the deck to make sure no one was watching him.

"Come on down in the cabin. Some of these stool pigeons might squeal on you," he said.

"Hey, sailors ain't allowed in the after quarters," I protested.

Svenson snarled something out of the corner of his mouth, and then he shook me by the shoulders.

"Do you want this candy or don't you?"

"Yes, I do."

"All right then, shut your trap and come on down below."

I followed him down into the chartroom. He made no show of giving me any box of candy.

"Where is it?" I asked.

Svenson held out a five pound box of candy wrapped in shiny paper and tied with lots of pink ribbon. I grabbed for it. As I did so he snatched it away just out of my reach.

"Oh no, you don't! Give me a kiss and you can have it."

"You said you'd give me the candy because you killed my fish." I couldn't understand why he still held the candy as another bait.

"Come on with the kiss or you don't get it," he insisted.

I looked at his tobacco-stained mouth and the yellow stubs of teeth that showed when he spoke. He looked horrible to me, but it was a five pound box of candy and it would be all my own and I had never had a whole pound of candy in my life, and I thought it would be worth even kissing Svenson for. I pursed my lips up to kiss him as I had kissed my father, my kittens and sea birds.

"Here's the kiss," I said.

He put his face down close to mine and I remember now how hot his breath was in my face. His mouth was twisted and his eyes narrowed and for years after in every horrible dream I ever had I saw Svenson's yellow teeth and narrowed eyes. . . .

I forgot the candy and turned to run. He made a noise in his throat like a snarling animal and grabbed me up in his arms. His face was against mine. He forced my mouth open and kissed me—horribly! One of his hairy arms nearly crushed my ribs and his big paws patted over my body as I kicked and struggled. With his face against mine I couldn't make a sound. I managed to get my fingers in his eyes and tried to push them in. Suddenly he dropped me so that I fell to the deck of the cabin and he ran out of the chartroom and up to the deck. I scrambled to my feet and scurried like a rat to my own cabin, slammed the door and threw myself on my bunk. There I beat my hands against the wall and bit into my straw pillow to keep from screaming.

I don't know how long it was before I felt Father's hands shaking me.

"For the love of Christ, what's the matter, Joan?" he kept saying above my muffled sobbing.

"Get out of here, I hate you! Get out of here! Get out!" I screeched at him. I didn't want to be touched; I just wanted to hide in the dark somewhere to get away from the feeling of Svenson's kiss.

Then I remembered the fish in my breast. I put my hand down and brought it out. When Father saw it he asked:

"Say, are you bawling over a dead fish?" He was annoyed at what he thought my childish sentiment. I didn't have time to answer him, for he left my cabin abruptly. I lay down again in the bunk clasping my dead bullfish and shivering with fear. Father came back with a big can of Epsom salts.

"Now, no more of this nonsense. What's the matter with you anyway? Are you sick?"

"No, Father, I just—I—" I couldn't finish for I knew the penalty of squealing on anyone in a fight. Sailors don't do that; they take their beating and settle with the offender at their leisure. I felt that if I told on Svenson I wouldn't be fit to be a regular sailor, and it was Father himself who had drilled that code into me.

"Answer me, are you sick, or is this just a show of bad temper?"

"I'm sick," I wailed in a weak voice. I knew what would follow. Father made me take a big dose of salts and then told me to go to bed.

"You don't get any supper. You probably been sneaking something to eat that wasn't good for you, so no food for you until we get your stomach cleaned up."

I didn't mind swallowing the salts, for it got Father away from me, and I was afraid I would tell him the truth if he asked me many more questions or accused me of being a blubbering child.

I didn't come out of my bunk all the next day. I stayed there with my fish. The fish began to smell bad so Father took it away from me and threw it out of the porthole.

That evening we sailed for the Midway Islands. I could hear the scuffling of the crew's feet on the poop deck above my cabin as they ran about setting the sails. The creak and groan of the rigging and the whistle of the wind through the sails gave me the creeps. Ordinarily the sound of our ship getting under way thrilled me, and I wasn't content unless I could be on deck helping pull the ropes. But I was afraid to go on deck. I heard Svenson's voice answering that of the mate's as he took the helm, and I couldn't bear to see him again.

When we had been out about a week, I ventured on deck, after I had found out from the cabin-boy that Svenson was on his watch below. I hated him but I was going to repay him in full when I got my courage back.

I knew to be a regular sailor I had to cure the sick feeling I got whenever Svenson was near. I had to quit being afraid; I had to get hunk without help. I couldn't even tell Stitches.

So I schemed and schemed, and I was so eager to get even that gradually I began to stop being afraid. The mate had switched Svenson into the second mate's watch because he wanted another sailor to fix some sails and Svenson couldn't sailmake. But he could steer. I found him at the wheel. Here was my chance! Just as I knew better than to squeal on him I was sure he would not dare to squeal on me, no matter what I did. Father had set a course, "Northeast by east, a quarter point east," and had told Svenson to keep a true course, for we were in the region of some coral reefs, and a quarter of a mile off in navigation would run us aground.

"Keep her full and by and call me if the wind veers a point," Father instructed him and then went below for a short nap. I knew if Svenson let that ship even get so much as a tenth of a point off the course that he would get hell from Father. Well, I'd help Svenson get his hell!

I climbed on the binnacle box (the box that holds the compass), which was in front of the wheel, and I put my two feet over the compass so that Svenson couldn't see it to steer by.

"Get the hell out of the way so I can see," he snarled at me.

"You make me!" I shot back at him. If he took his hands off the helm the rudder would spin around and the ship would be out of control. "Come on, make me get off this binnacle," I invited him again. Svenson knew I had him. He lost his temper and began cursing me, but he kept to the wheel..I heard the topsails aloft begin to flap. The wind had caught them "aback." The jibs and mainsails began to luff—and in vain Svenson spun the wheel to get the ship back on her course. Then it was my turn to laugh. I heard the mate, on the fo'c's'le head where he was fixing a jib, bellow aft at Svenson to pull the goddamned ship back into the wind. The mate ran down the deck to help get her back on course. He wasn't fast enough though, for Father, who had been watching his telltale compass over his bunk, was leaping up the companionway ladder to the poop. I ran to the windward rail and pretended I was interested in watching some schools of flying fish skim over the water. Father jerked the helm from Svenson's hand and spun it hard over to leeward. With a slapping crash the booms went over to the port tack, and he got her once more headed up to the wind.

"Joan, take this wheel," he ordered. I came over and took hold of its big spokes. "Show this cock-eyed so and so sea louse how to steer a course," he said out of the corner of his mouth, and at that he grabbed Svenson.

"Who in the hell ever told you you were a sailor? What do you mean by letting her run afoul in the wind?" He shouted in Svenson's face.

"That ain't my fault, Captain," whispered back Svenson. "I couldn't help it."

"You'll talk back to me, will you?" and Father sent him flying on the deck with a left uppercut: "Trying to run the goddamned ship on a reef for us, are you?" Svenson jumped to his feet and went for Father.

"Why you white-haired old bastard, I'll knock the so

and so out of you," and he swung a fierce right to Father's head. Then the two of them wallowed around the deck, punching and mauling each other in a bloody mess. I'll never forget the sound of the bones in Svenson's jaw crunching under Father's blows.

"I've got enough!" cried Svenson, on his back, just as Father's upraised arm was about to put him to sleep. The mate, who was standing by with a belaying pin in his hand in case of real trouble, lifted the Norwegian to his feet.

"Take him for'ard, and put him in irons," Father ordered the mate, "and tell any of the crew in the fo'c's'le that think they can talk back to the captain of this ship that Svenson is only a sample of what'll happen to them."

The mate had Svenson by the neck and the seat of his pants marching him forward. Father called after them: "When that piece of ballast gets his eyes open again, I'll have Joan here show him how to steer a ship."

Svenson, however, was kept in irons and on rations of bread and water until we reached the Midway Islands, where Father discharged him in disgrace—I hadn't squealed, but I don't think Svenson, wherever he is to-day, feels that he got the best of it.

7

A runaway sea horse

MY days at sea were divided up between work, study and play. In fair weather my schedule was crowded. At seven-thirty in the morning I got my breakfast. At eight bells, when the morning watch came on duty, I had to swab down the poop deck, polish the brass work and make up my bunk. My bunk was graced by a mattress of "donkey's breakfast" or straw, which was the nearest thing to material luxury I ever knew. I never worked very hard at my duties; rather I made them into games whenever I could.

I had to haul up water in a canvas bucket to wash down the decks. I liked that because it gave me the chance to use the bucket to catch things that floated by. Sometimes this led to adventures I had not foreseen.

I'll always remember the morning I tried to catch the sea horse. A sea horse sounds very formidable for a ten-year-old girl to go after with a canvas bucket because naturally when one says "sea horse" many people com-

pare it to a huge clumsy sea animal weighing hundreds
of pounds. But the sea horse is quite different. He is a
funny fish from two or three inches to a foot long. I call
him a funny fish because for a fish he can't swim any
more than a cockroach, but he has a tail that he wraps
about a piece of seaweed or any drifting thing. So he
meanders over the ocean with his head out of water at
such an angle that from a short distance he looks like a
horse's head—hence his name.

It is only about once in a blue moon that any sailor
catches a sea horse, so of course at ten it was the dream
of my life to land one.

What a thrill it was that morning when leaning over
the side, bucket in hand, I saw floating just beneath me
a sea anemone on which was a tiny sea horse riding as if
the sea flower was its throne, and the sea horse was king
of the ocean. What an opportunity! The morning was
calm, the flat sea like glass, and the lazy ship crawling
along at scarcely three knots an hour made fishing conditions ideal. The sea horse was a transparent, gelatine-
looking blue. I could see the tiny threads of blue veins in
its insides. I lowered the bucket under the anemone and
started to haul it up, but the water carried it floating off.
I threw the bucket at it again. In the foam it had disappeared. I watched carefully and was rewarded by seeing it reappear again near the stern of the ship. I ran
to the taffrail and plunged the bucket again after it, but
missed it by about two feet. There was not time to pull
up the bucket and make another cast. The stern of the
moving ship would pass the drifting anemone. I saw my
life's ambition slipping away from me. I wouldn't fail!

That miss gave me a wild desire to possess the sea horse

or die in the attempt to get it. Without a thought as to the utter foolishness of what I was doing I jumped over-board after the sea horse! When I landed with a splash in the water I heard Stitches' voice shout:

"The skipper's overboard!"

Such a hullabaloo that started on deck. Father had come up, the cabin-boy, Bulgar and Axel Oleson. They were huddled at the stern rail. The mate and Swede were unfastening the leachings on the dinghy to lower it over after me.

"Keep your head up, Skipper," called Stitches in a frantic voice. He couldn't swim a stroke and his help-lessness to aid me as he wanted to was funny. He kept calling instructions to me.

The wake of the vessel was washing the sea horse far-ther away from me. Instead of swimming back to the ship and grabbing hold of the life line that Father threw after me, I swam lickety-split astern after my prize—the ship going on in one direction and I in the other. I never got many opportunities to get off the ship and I was exhilarated at my freedom. I was free—my goal was the rapidly fleeing sea flower. I knew I would achieve my ambition!

"Tread water," came the bellowing voice of my father through his cupped hands. "Don't get scared and you'll be all right."

I turned my head to look at him, sent him a smile, waved my hand at him and plunged on after my flower. I would no sooner swim within easy reach of it, so I thought, than a gentle wave lapped it out of my grasp. I forgot the gang on the ship who were trying to call me back. With several swift strokes I overtook the sea horse on its flower chariot. I grabbed it in my fist. The anemone crushed in my hand. Triumphant at catching it I turned back to catch up with the ship. Father had hove to in the little wind that was wheezing out of some straggling clouds. The mate was in the lifeboat with Stitches and Bulgar. They were pulling for dear life after me. With the thrill of my success still tingling in my soul I decided to give the men in the lifeboat some work. I had jumped overboard with my overalls on, so stuffing my prize in my front pocket I turned about and began swimming away. I swam as fast as I could. The men in the lifeboat pulled with longer and swifter strokes. I plowed on a few yards and then turned and waved a hand to them to come and get me. I heard them begin to curse the air blue. I trod water until they almost got up with me, then I dived under the water, and came up a few yards behind them and started back to the ship. By the time they got the lifeboat turned around I was way ahead. It wasn't every day in my life that I was important enough to get the whole crew off duty to chase me around the ocean and I was making the most of it!

When I got under the shadow of the stern, just far enough away to clear the suction of the rudder, I looked up to the deck and saw the crew laughing—that is, they were all laughing with the exception of my father.

"That damned old sea horse thought he could get away from me but I got him," I called up, grinning in my success.

"Come up this rope at once," roared Father.

Hand over hand I climbed up the piece of halyard he lowered over to me. My hair was streaked in wet strings over my face as I stood on deck dripping in front of

Father. Before he could say a word I put my hand in my pocket to bring out my beautiful anemone when to my dismay the thing I brought forth in my fist was no dainty colored flower but a dirty piece of seaweed that looked like a hunk of rotten sponge. In the water in its bed of blue sea it had the beauty of a lace-like piece of coral, but in my hand it was a brutal disillusion—just ugly seaweed. My heart sank in disappointment—the thing I had wanted to possess for its loveliness didn't exist. Whatever philosophic reflections this might have started were checked abruptly by my father's voice.

"Turn over that skylight," he said.

Obediently I draped my body over the skylight with my back part exposed heavenwards.

"This will teach you to run away from this ship," and he gave me a whipping with the end of the rope he had thrown to me to climb aboard with. The licking didn't really hurt. It took a pretty healthy whack to hurt me anywhere physically. But the comedown! The blow to my pride! To be turned over a skylight and licked on the pants before a circle of grinning sailors—and for what? Merely for jumping overboard in mid-ocean and stopping the ship. I could hear the mate who had chased me in the lifeboat laughing the loudest. Would I ever recover? As if the sea horse and the anemone hadn't treated me badly enough.

"Now you get the Bible and copy a verse twenty times," he added. It was the familiar finish to a licking. Father used the Bible as a text book for me—spelling, grammar and composition. If you've ever had to learn to spell all the words in the Bible you can see what I was up against. I had to copy verses out of the Bible every day, but Father could never make me do it voluntarily —so he gave it to me to do as punishment.

I got the Bible, and lying down on my stomach on the hot deck in the sun so my pants would dry, I began my penmanship lesson. I was darned if I was going to do Revelations again. I knew them by heart—all about roasting in Hell and being eaten by snakes and never being able to die and get out of it—besides which the verses in Revelations were too long. I wanted to get it over with. I thumbed the New Testament over until I found the shortest verse in it—"Jesus Wept." That suited my frame of mind too, so I copied that one twenty times and turned my homework in to Father. He was so pleased at my promptness in doing my lesson that he looked as if he had forgotten my latest offense.

"Here it is," I said to him, with the air of a martyr, and disdaining even to look at that bunch of sailors who were occupied doing various jobs around the deck. As I handed him the paper I began to make a discreet retreat to the main deck. I got as far as the poop deck ladder when I heard him explode like a firecracker. And then I got a real licking to "teach me to be funny again."

Studying was the hardest thing I had to do. It wasn't only because I didn't want to study that I looked upon knowledge-getting as a curse, but I had so much physical energy that I just couldn't sit still long enough. So Father used all sorts of schemes to make me work at my lessons. He had one that never failed, no matter how often he tried it. He would call me into his cabin and tell me with a grave face he had made a mistake in his navigation problem and would I work it over and catch his mistake, because otherwise the result might be very serious to all of us on the ship. I didn't care a hang about the seriousness to all of us on the ship, but how I did want to catch him. So I would tie into that problem tooth and nail and at the end of half an hour or an hour be able to go to Father with a very superior air and tell him that no matter what he thought I knew he had *not* made a mistake. Then he'd always thank me with an expression of great relief and I'd go away very proud—never realizing that I had done my arithmetic lesson.

There was always plenty of work for me to do, but nothing for me to play with that I didn't invent myself. Father always said:

"I don't have playthings—why should you?"

Left to my own resources I copied my few toys from the things I saw around me—sailors, ships and cargoes. I built a drydock under the ladder leading to the poop. In my drydock I had several types of ships in the making. My prize ship was a full-rigger in a whiskey bottle. The sailors had taught me to make long crochet hooks from bits of wire and to make my own glue from fish heads.

I worked for months making the parts of the ship to rig up. Then came the problem of getting it inside the narrow neck of the whiskey bottle and setting it up inside. That was where the crochet hooks came in. I put all the parts of the full-rigger in the bottle separately and then I put them into place with the use of the glue and hooks. I worked a little every day on my masterpiece for I wanted it to be superior to any bottle boat that could be produced in the fo'c's'le. Eventually I had built a fleet of little ships. I made them to trade in English ports for candy.

My most spectacular vessel, however, was a boat that sailed on the deck on little wooden wheels. It was about two feet long with a mainsail, squaresail and two jibs. I made the diminutive blocks in its rigging from bits of sandalwood. The mainsail and squaresail were fashioned from an old cotton shirt, while its jibs had once been a pair of underdrawers which the cook cast off.

Stitches made a boat on the same model and on the day both were completed we were to have a race. My boat was called the *Neversink*. Stitches' boat was the *Sonofabitch*.

"I'll wager you my boat'll outsail yours, Skipper," he said. "An' if I lose you can embroider the name of your winner, the *Neversink,* in white twine on my pants' seat, an' I'll wear the same for every man aboard to see."

"That's a bet, Stitches," I said, taking his wager. Unfortunately I didn't stop to consider that if his boat won he would embroider its name, *Sonofabitch,* on the back of me.

Came the day of the race. It was the rule that we had to man our boats with a crew—the owner having the sole pick of whatever kind of crew he desired. The captain of my boat was a fat cockroach. I tied him to his post aft with a piece of thread. However I never called much attention to him in my father's hearing for fear Father would think there was something personal about it. You see, I learned early that a girl can't be too careful with a man's dignity. My "crew" was a kitten which I tied on just forward of midships to serve the double purpose of crew and ballast to hold the *Neversink* on deck when the wind blew its sails. As in all well-regulated ships I had trouble with my crew.

We had our boats at the starting line on the main deck. The goal was the water tank abaft the mizzen.

"Shove off!" signalled Stitches and down the decks the *Neversink* and the *Sonofabitch* careened along on their wheels. My boat took the lead and kept a couple of inches ahead of the *Sonofabitch,* when my crew mutinied. The wind got under the kitten's tail and he didn't like it so he clawed at the sails and pulled the mast and rigging down, finally dumping the *Neversink* over on her side in dismal defeat.

I didn't wait for Stitches to gloat over his victory.

"You can have my overalls when I turn in tonight but don't embroider *Sonofabitch* in too big letters," I said.

Sometimes my games got me in trouble, and once I was badly injured. On the "dog watches" from four to six and six to eight in the evenings, both watches were on deck and I didn't have to keep quiet so they could sleep. It was then that I ran the decks, careless of the thudding noise my feet made; or I sang chanteys loud and long at the top of my voice. One night I persuaded Swede to play tag with me. Owing to the limited space there is on a ship to run around in, we made a rule that the person who was "it" had to catch the pursued by hitting him three hard swats in the middle of the back. There were no bases. The topmasts were the limit above and the hold the limit below. I was it. I chased Swede forward, through the galley, back to the mizzen, around the mizzen mast, over the hatchway and almost caught him when he leaped to the shrouds and started up the mizzen rigging. I went after him with a rush. He was about half way up the ratlines when I almost overtook him. Instead of continuing up and sliding down a halyard to the deck again from the cross-trees as I thought he would, he stopped short in the rigging.

"Get down or I'll step on your hands," he said with a grin.

"Step away and be damned," I answered him, intent on catching him at any cost. Of course a huge Swede sailor is not the most gentle playmate there is for a child, but he was all that was available. In his clumsiness he was only playing, but he raised one foot as if to trample on my hands and said again:

"Get down or you get me hoof on your mitts."

I didn't believe he meant it, so instead of taking his warning I went up another rung of the rigging. He intended to step lightly but he slipped. I felt a stinging pain and then I was flying through space. I suppose my hands went out as protection instinctively for they struck the deck first. Something seemed to snap in both wrists and my face slapped against the planks of the deck.

The next thing I knew Swede had me in his arms lugging me aft and I was kicking and blubbering cross words through bloody lips. It was bad enough to be smashed up but to be carried like a helpless puppy was too much.

"Put me down," I demanded and I wriggled from his arms. Mustering all the strength I could I walked up the poop. Father had come up the companionway to investigate the commotion. When he saw me he asked:

"Now what the hell have you been up to?"

My face evidently looked like a muffin that had spilled over lopsided in baking, for my nose was broken and two points off its course.

"Answer me. What happened?" Father repeated with force.

"I guess I've busted my flippers. Can you fix them?" was all I could reply.

He took my broken wrists in his hands and examined them, then sent the man at the wheel after a fruit box.

"Now you get below, Joan. I'll make some splints out of slats of wood and set your arms. But about your nose, how in the hell can I do anything with that?"

Despite his doubts, Father made a good job of patching me up. He used a ruler broken in two pieces for a splint for my nose, and then put a finishing touch on his handiwork by giving me a big dose of salts. Father sincerely believed salts were a cure for everything from bad temper to a broken neck, and I became so inured to swallowing the darn stuff that I almost learned to like it.

8

We catch a female shark and I learn about women from her—

ONE of the earliest lessons that I learned from the sea was the importance of observation. Book learning is almost useless in a storm, and science an unknown quantity when the elements lash against a man-built ship. But observing the laws of the sea, watching it destroy or create, teaches much about life. All that I learned of philosophy, biology and astronomy came to me from my father and the sailors.

I often wondered where children came from, and in reply to my queries the sailors gave me no stork fable or yarn about being found in a cabbage patch. When I asked Father where I came from he replied:

"Don't ask questions. Just keep your eyes open and you'll find out everything you want to know."

The first opportunity I had to find out about babies being born came when Father landed a shark. I was down on the main deck helping Stitches sew on a ripped sail. He was teaching me how to use the "palm" or sea-going thimble that sailors use when they sew canvas. The "palm" is a metal perforated disk set on a leather strap that fits the palm of the hand. In fair weather the sailors always brought the torn sails on deck and repaired them ready for emergency use in a storm. Stitches was very painstaking in his instruction to me because he wanted me to be a regular sailor some day.

Father was sitting on the taffrail, sextant in hand, waiting for the sun to come out from behind a cloud so that he could "shoot the sun," or take a sight to figure out our position by navigation.

"Say, Joan," he called, "come here and look at this shark."

I dropped my sewing and ran up to the poop to the after rail. I looked over the stern and saw a greenish white shadow deep in the water. Slowly the shadow came closer to the surface and a grey fin stuck out of the water like a three-cornered sail. The shark was about ten feet long. It swam around in circles following in our wake, stalking us. It was the first time I had ever seen a man-eating shark.

"Don't go too near the rail, Joan. If you fall overboard now you'll be a nice dessert for that shark."

"Do sharks eat people?" I asked.

"That kind of a shark does. All sharks that live on the surface of the water and follow sailing ships are man-eaters."

I looked at the shark again. It looked harmless to me as it circled and played around in the wake from our rudder.

"How could a shark eat me? I can't see any mouth on it," I countered, still unconvinced.

"I'll show you. Go ask the cook for a big chunk of salt pork, and we'll put it on an iron hook, then watch the fun."

I got the chunk of salt pork and Father baited a hook with it. Instead of lowering the hook overboard by a rope, he fastened a thin chain about twenty feet long onto it.

"Now get my rifle, and stand clear of the rail," he ordered.

I brought the gun up, and Stitches and McLean came aft to help land the shark. Stitches tied a piece of board on the chain so that the pork and hook would float on the surface. The shark, led by its little vari-colored pilot fish, smelled at the bait—then it circled away. It came back again and after pushing the pork with its snout, the shark turned belly up, and opened its jaws on the meat. A shark can only bite when it is bottom up, as the lower part of its jaw is receding. As it turned up and snagged the hook Father shot at his throat with his rifle. The shark kicked out with its powerful tail and pulled away. McLean let out some slack as the shark started to bite viciously at the chain holding the hook. Again and again Father fired shots into its body, but still it fought. The pilot fish had disappeared—nothing remained but a bleeding, fighting shark pulling at the hook.

"Haul him up, head out of water," Father called, and as Stitches and McLean pulled him out of the water Father slipped a running bowline around him.

"Get the hell out of the way now or you'll get hurt," he called to me as he hauled the heavy shark up by the bowline. Stitches had slipped another line around the shark's pounding tail and was pulling him up by the stern. After a terrific struggle they landed him on the poop deck. It slapped and wallowed around the deck, its huge jaws with seven rows of saw-teeth gaping and trying to kill its attackers. Father ran a scantline down its throat and shot it again. McLean chopped its tail off, splintering its spine as he did so. Still the shark fought desperately. Nothing seemed to kill it.

"A shark don't die until sundown," said my father, "but we can cut him up so he can't do any damage. Only don't get too near him because he may only be foxing. A shark is the hardest deep sea thing to kill there is."

Father told the men to haul the body of the shark down on the main deck and leave it in the lee scuppers until it died. The sailors were more than willing to comply because a shark has a lot of value to sailormen.

"When it's dead, you men skin it. We'll sell the skin in Australia for shoe leather. Whatever else you want of the shark you can have," he told the men, and he went about his task of "shooting the sun."

I forgot all about my sail sewing lesson in the excitement of carving up a man-eating shark. Stitches sharpened my knife for me on his marlin spike, and we set about carving up the shark.

"What part can I do?" I asked him.

"Well, seeing as this is the first man-eating shark you ever seen caught, you go through its guts. Some sailors tell as how sharks swallow pearls on the bottom of the ocean, and maybe if you was to carefully go through all its entrails you might find a pearl."

It is true that sharks are the scavengers of the underseas, but Stitches gave me the job of looking through its guts to initiate me into the realm of sharkdom. "Nothing like learning the insides of things to be sure of your facts," he said.

I am glad now that he made me go through that shark's insides for it gave me first hand information that has backed me up when landlubbers doubt me when I tell them of the mammal shark.

It took about three hours to go carefully through the yards and yards of gut of that shark and I didn't find any pearls. All I found was a rusty piece of tin and a small devil fish, or octopus, that spit indigo ink all over me when I freed it from the grip of the shark.

"I'm goin' to cut out this backbone, Skipper, and make a walking stick out of it. I can sell it when I get ashore for a bottle of rum," said Stitches, and he dug his knife into the back of the shark. The shark still quivered, hacked up as it was.

"And now let's get his ugly mug off his body. His yawnin' jaws look too hungry for comfort." McLean got an ax and a saw, and the two of them sawed and hacked off the huge iron-like head.

"Now I'll show you where the shark keeps his eyes." You see, a shark is blind, it can only see about four inches in front of its snout. Every shark has two little parasite fish, pilot fish, that see for it, and in time of trouble the shark swallows its pilot fish for protection. Down in little sockets behind the shark's gills, Stitches brought out two squirming, brightly colored fish, about three inches long.

People have often asked me how it is that natives seem to swim unharmed in shark-infested waters. They escape from death because they know a shark's habits. A shark, by reason of its near-sightedness, depends upon its pilot fish to spot food for it. The tiny fish can see any animate

object in the water and head for it. The bright color of
their bodies shines in front of the shark who follows
where they lead. A shark will not attack an inanimate object for it cannot notice it! A moving object in the water
attracts attention and the natives, wise to this, let their
bodies go limp when a shark circles too near them. Then,
when a shark circles to turn around to attack, the native
moves like lightning to dive under the animal and rip
its throat with his sharp tortoise-shell knife.

"Now always remember, Skipper, if you ever are overboard and near a shark, keep your head and keep quiet
until the shark circles from you. Don't be a landlubber
fool and try to fight because that just makes you a movin'
target fer the little pilot fish." I have been laughed at
when I have told about the pilot fish of a shark, and un-
believers have said it was just a good fish yarn, but never-
theless it is a fact.

"Do any other kind of fish eat you, too?" I asked, a
bit worried.

"Hell, a shark ain't a fish, it's a mammal—just like a
porpoise and a whale is a mammal."

A shark not a fish? It had fins and a body and tail like
one and it doesn't have to come up to the surface to
breathe like a porpoise and a whale.

"Now you take that shark jaw and hang it over the
side in the water and in a week all the meat will rot off
it; then you'll have a pair of fine shark's jaws to hang up
in your cabin."

No portion of that shark was to be wasted. McLean
had taken the empty gut and had stretched it out in the
sun to dry. "For shoelaces" he answered, when I asked
him what he was keeping it for.

"But it stinks," I protested.

"Well, it won't when I cure it in salt," he replied.

"Now we'll cut its stomach open, Skipper," said Stitches and he slit up the upper stomach of the mutilated shark. I bent over him, carefully watching everything he did, for wonders never ceased to come from it.

Stitches reached his hand and wrist into the opening and felt inside. Then he let forth a "Jesus!"

"What's the matter, Stitches?"

"Skipper," he replied, his face crestfallen, "this is a mother shark. Look, she has young 'uns in her."

I looked, and there in a pouch in her stomach were six baby sharks, about eighteen inches long. He reached in deeper and brought out a second pouch with another litter of six young in it.

"Is it bad luck to kill a she-shark, Stitches?" I asked, puzzled at his sudden grief.

"Bad luck? No sailor ever kills a female thing, because they give life. Givin' life is part of the Creator's job, and no man would willingly kill a mother thing."

There is an old superstition that to kill any female thing at sea will bring a curse on the ship. If a female bird is killed, its wing is nailed on the mast head as an offering against a curse. When Stitches saw we had killed a mother shark in young, he took the tail and nailed it on the end of the jib boom. That is the reason why ships returning from deep sea voyages are often decorated with parts of birds or fish.

After Stitches had put up the tail on the jib boom, he came back to the shark. "Maybe we can save these young 'uns, Skipper." Carefully, and almost tenderly, he took the baby fish out of the pouch and broke the cords that

bound them to the mother shark. Then he took some twine
that he had been using to sew sails with, and tied up the
end of each cord, and threw the little fish overboard.
They probably never lived but Stitches did everything in
his power to save them.

I didn't know that sharks bore their young. I supposed
they laid spawn as any other fish did, but Stitches explained to me that a shark bears her children like a human, and suckles them from a teat until they can forage
for their own food. The reason that shark had fought so
viciously was to protect the young in her. A male shark
is much easier to land, and much more stupid than a female.

I asked Stitches if all children were born the way the
sharks were and he answered, yes.

As there were eleven children in our family I thought
that we came in batches of six like the sharks.

"But how do we get in the pouches?" I insisted.

"The guy that created you put the seed of you under
your father's and your mother's heart, then when they
fell in love you was born."

I have since learned that some modern naturalists who
evidently never have traveled further south than Sandy
Hook, have expressed a doubt as to whether there really
is such a beast as a man-eating shark and whether it will
actually attack a man unprovoked. Evidence, they claim,
has always been at second-hand and the testimony of sea-
faring men they reject. Well, without wishing to lock
horns with the learned, you may be interested in first-
hand evidence of man-eating sharks.

I saw a nurse shark, perhaps the deadliest species of
the shark family, attack a sailor from our ship, one Eric

Johanssen. Johanssen dived off the ship for a swim against the express command of my father that no member of the crew leave the vessel. We were anchored in Paramatta River in Sydney Harbor. Johannsen hadn't been in the water five minutes before two sharks began circling about him.

"You bloody fool, swim for the ship," called Swede to Johannsen. Johanssen turned to strike out for the Jacob's ladder, but he wasn't swift enough. The tricornered fin of the biggest shark followed in his wake. Johannsen struck out wildly with his arms and legs. He evidently thought that by making a big splash in the water he would confuse the shark, but the disturbance Johanssen kicked up only served to make an accurate target for the shark's pilot fish.

The man had about reached the ship when the triangular fin following disappeared. Watching, the men on board knew what that meant. The brute was turning on its back. It came up below its prey and turned open its huge maw to bite.

There came a short shriek of pain; the water bloodied, and Johanssen's body doubled up. The shark's jaws had set about his stomach. With a sinuous motion of its tail the shark drew away taking in its jaws the middle of Johanssen's body almost through to the backbone.

There had been no time to lower a boat, but Swede was on the Jacob's ladder; Father and the mate above, all the boathooks fighting to save at least the body from the man-eaters. They caught the body with their hooks and brought it out, but not until another hunk of flesh had been torn from the thigh. Then the vicious monsters, balked of their complete meal, swam along the sides of the ship, scraping against it and slapping their tails against the hull as though in a frenzy of rage. Finally they drew off, but for hours they swam close by, waiting for another victim.

Father had Johanssen's body sewn up in sailcloth and it was buried in the potter's field in Sydney.

Stitches told me of a foolhardy sailor in the islands dragging his arm over the side of a dinghy going ashore. A nurse shark came up unexpectedly and caught the trailing arm. The sailor either was dragged, or in his fright fell out of the boat. There was a swirl of bloody water and the man was gone. Then, attracted by the blood another huge shark came alongside and scraped the dinghy trying to overturn it. Stitches and the remaining sailor had a hard time getting the boat safely ashore.

Such are the habits of man-eating sharks.

9

In which I learn to take a joke. Hoping you may do the same

WE were nearing the Equator bound south from Puget Sound. Father, the mate, and I were eating our noon meal, "onion bouillon" (one bucket of water with one onion in it), rice with curry sauce and boiled tapioca with pale lavender cornstarch sauce. The Jap cook delighted in coloring the food to make it appear more appetizing than it was.

Father and the mate were discussing our position on the chart.

"We ought to make the crossing along about four bells this afternoon, Mr. Swanson. Better get the big hawser out and stretch it on deck in case we need it."

The mate caught the twinkle in Father's eye and raised his voice for the benefit of the greenhorn cabin-boy who was listening to the conversation, big-eyed, in the pantry.

"All right, Captain, and when Neptune comes aboard shall I tell him about Slops trespassing on his domain?"

"Yes. He'll probably raise hell because he doesn't like the uninitiated to cross the Equator."

The cabin-boy came out of the pantry and made a pretense of passing the bread to me.

"I beg your pardon, sir," he said to Father, "but what does the Equator look like?"

"It's a white line about three feet under the water. I just told Mr. Swanson here to get out the hawser and have it ready. When we cross the Equator we begin goin' down hill and slip south so fast we got to tie a line on to the Equator," Father lied without blinking an eye.

Slops sniffed, pretending contempt.

"You can't fool me, Captain," he protested.

Father looked very stern.

"When you have washed up here I want you to lean overboard and look for the line and when you see it, call me," he ordered the cabin-boy.

Slops' eyes nearly popped out of his sallow face, but he claimed that he didn't believe it.

When Father and the mate left the table and went on deck, Slops came to me.

"Does the Old Man mean that stuff about us going too fast when we cross the Equator?" he asked.

"Sure he does, and what's more, Neptune knows you've never crossed the line before, and you're going to be tarred and feathered," I promised him. "Besides that, you'll probably have to clean up all the mess they make tarring and feathering you."

Slops didn't think so much of me at that moment, and he turned back to his pantry with a sniff. An hour later Father asked me where Slops had disappeared to. I didn't know, but I set about to find him. I looked in the pantry, in his cabin, up in the galley, under the fo'c's'le-head, aloft in the rigging, down in the lazarette, everywhere, so I thought, and I couldn't track him. We were just about to cross the Equator, and Slops' presence was desired on deck for the initiation. Mr. Swanson stepped up to my father!

"Come with me, Captain, and I'll show you where that cat-livered cabin-boy is." I went with them, forward, and there we found Slops. He was leaning far out the hawse hole staring at the water below looking for the Equator! The mate planted his foot in the hind part of the cabin-boy and nearly sent him hurling into space through the hawse hole.

"Get amidships, you so and so ignoramus." Poor Slops, quaking with fear, ambled aft. There on the mizzen hatch he saw a platform built of timber on which was a big wooden tub of "shaving lather." The sailors were sitting around the tub on their haunches with treacherous innocence on their faces.

"Tie up the beggar," ordered Swede, who had assumed charge of the activities. Slops was grabbed by Bulgar and McLean and bound hand and foot with rope. For a moment there was an ominous pause, and then slowly coming down off the fo'c's'le head was old Neptune himself. One of the sailors had rigged himself up in a torn gunny sack, with long, straggly beard made of rope yarn and he carried a trident. It is the custom for the Captain of the ship to turn over all authority to Neptune when crossing the Line. Neptune took his stand on the wooden platform. He called for silence, and then his voice boomed out, .

"Where is the son of a bitch that dares trespass my Equator without his passport?"

McLean and Swede shoved Slops in front of Neptune.

"This is the offender, sir," said Swede.

Neptune looked at him condemningly. He took the old stubble paintbrush in his hand and dipped it into the lather. We all knew just what was in that lather!

"What is your name?" roared Neptune.

Slops opened his mouth to tell his name and Neptune put some of the lather off the brush into it. The sailors laughed heartily at Slops' discomfiture. The tar in the lather stuck to his face, and when it was at the proper gluey stickiness to hold the "feather," Neptune threw dried copra on him. It stuck fast and gave Slops the appearance of a wild ape. He tried to resist Neptune and that made his lot worse, for the sailors, as a punishment for his insubordination, fastened a long rope to his body and threw him overboard. They dragged him along until he was almost unconscious and then hauled him on deck.

"Let's splice the mainbrace, Neptune," said Father, and he opened a bottle of rum. Each man got a big swig out of it, but Slops got only a smell of the cork.

I was laughing so hard at the whole performance that I was oblivious of the preparations of Neptune to lather some one else. I was not to be kept in ignorance for long.

"Captain," bawled Neptune, "has your daughter got her passport for crossing the Line?"

"Say, I crossed the Equator when I was a year old, and they never did anything to me because I was a baby," I bragged, "and besides that, I've crossed about twenty times." I swelled my chest out and bulged my muscles in true sailor fashion, so cocky was I about being a regular old salt.

"You ain't been initiated, huh? Well, Captain, it's about time she was. What about it?" he asked. Father looked at me as if he was full of pity for my predicament, and then in a half-mocking, sad tone he said,

"Guess she'll have to get tarred and feathered, too."

"Hey, what the hell?" I piped up.

"This is the what," said Neptune. "You're next," and he waved to the tub of lather.

"Just try and do it," I challenged him, really getting sore. It had ceased to be funny to me, and the more excited I got the funnier it seemed to the sailors.

"You cock-eyed quart of bilgewater, you haven't got a chance of tarring and keelhauling me," I snorted and jumped for the rigging. I got no farther. Swede dragged me back by the foot. They bound me as they had the luckless Slops and applied the brush and lather to my face.

"What is your name, little girl?" cooed that damned Neptune. I was too wise to open my mouth, so I thought, for I had no intention of swallowing any of that concoction.

"Answer me," he bellowed.

I closed my lips tighter. Huh, I was smarter than they were after all. I'd show them! "Smack" on my behind went a plank, heaved by the ape-like Slops. It was such a hard whack that I opened my mouth to holler, and no sooner had I done that than Neptune stuck a big gob of lather in the wide aperture of my jaws, and then I heard the whole crew and my father guffawing at me. Slops had been initiated, so he rated disciplining me. From head to foot they soaked me in that lather. The tar in it

matted my long thick hair together and stuck my eye-
lashes so that I couldn't open my eyes. I wouldn't have
minded it so much if I hadn't heard them all laughing at
me.

When no more lather would stick to me I heard Father
say to Neptune:

"Let's throw her over and give her a bath. She's so
dirty now that she'll just love it." What I thought of
my father and the whole bunch at that moment cannot be
written here, but it was very graphic!

Overboard I went, tied by the same rope that had been
on Slops. The salt water has the interesting effect of
making tar stick so that it will not come off without turpentine. When they thought I had had enough of a
bath, they hauled me out and sprinkled me with some
dried copra. I looked worse than Slops did. I sat in the
scupper picking off the shreds of coconut husks that
came in the copra, and I gave the appearance of a she-
orang outang picking off fleas.

As they say in the movies, time passed, but not my
temper. The copra I picked off stuck to my fingers. I
picked that off with the other hand and it stuck to the
other. It was a thankless job. And then there was my hair.
Never in this world would the tar come out of it. I went
to my ally, the cook, and asked him for some oil to rub
on me. He wouldn't give me any for he was afraid the
sailors would jump on him if he helped me.

"Well, at least you might give me some turpentine," I
said to the mate.

"Sure, all you want," and he gave me a five gallon tin
of it. "Now go ahead and enjoy yourself," he said. I

rubbed turpentine on the tar and it came off, but with it large pieces of my own skin.

"How in the hell will I get this stuff out of my hair?" I wailed.

"That's very simple, Joan; I guess I'll have to shave your hair off," said Father. He promptly set about to do it. With a carving knife he cut my long hair off, then he shaved my head with his razor. I was as sunburned as walnut juice, but my scalp was white, and the two-color tone of my face and head gave me the weird appearance of a native ready for a war dance.

I was not going to forget that little initiation party in a hurry. I didn't overlook any opportunity to get even with the sailors, Slops, the mate and my father during the rest of the trip.

I lay for Slops near the poop deck ladder one day when he was to bring the dinner basket aft. As he started to mount the ladder, I tripped him and sent the basket and the dinner flying over the deck. I caught some bed-bugs and put them in my father's and the mate's bunks, and to make sure the bugs would stay in them and bear millions of other little bedbugs, I stuck brown sugar in the ticking in their mattresses. It was not so easy for me to get even with the sailors, for I had no excuse to be in the fo'c's'le. About a month after the Equator episode I got my chance. It was a Sunday. We were in the trade winds and there was no ship work to be done. The sailors had one of those rare days at sea, to loaf. I'd show them how long they could loaf. Taking my penknife, I sneaked to the mizzen boom and pretended I was just swinging on it. I was really ripping the stitching in the middle of the sail. The wind caught in the little hole, and I ran and hid below, when I heard it start to rip. The force of the wind tore the sail right up to the gaff, and before Father saw it in time to lower it, the sail was in ribbons.

"All hands on deck!" he shouted. Away from their naps and pipes came the sailors. The ruined sail put the ship out of control, so Father had to heave to. "All hands on deck until a new sail is made," he ordered, and amid cursing and grumbling, far into the night, they sweated and slaved, getting up the new mizzen. That is, all hands, except me. I sat on the windward rail laughing at them.

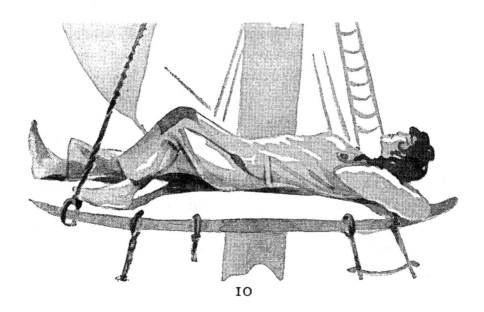

10

A bucko Captain and his Bible chart for me the mysteries of sex

"JOAN, when you've learned to take a licking without a squawk outta you, when you can lose something you've wanted for a long time and not be discouraged, when you can be becalmed for weeks in the doldrums without sight of the sun or a star to navigate by and not lose your faith in God Almighty because you can't understand His wisdom in confusing you—then you can go."

It was Father, for the dozenth time answering my question:

"Will I always have to be on a ship and never live in cities ashore?"

I am still, in my father's eyes, his baby girl, but how he fought to keep maturity from catching up with me! He never in my life fondled me affectionately—never held me and kissed me as fathers of little girls ashore do. He was afraid of making me hungry for the tender attentions that women give, and as there was no woman on board to give those attentions, he hardened me against them. He has told me since that he often ached to crush me to him when some childish thing I did made him realize how utterly lonely I was. One day he saw Stitches stroking my dark curls lovingly, and it was only Stitches' age that kept Father from beating him up. He sent Stitches to the fo'c's'le on rations of bread and water for three days with the warning that if he ever got soft-hearted over me again he'd have to take his sea bag to some other ship! When Father showed me affection he usually did it with a good hard kick or a hearty punch on the back such as men use to express emotion to each other without detracting from their manliness.

If Father believed in the wisdom of a rope's end on my southernmost portion to discipline me, he didn't neglect my character building. In spite of his roughness—his bellowing voice to the sailors in a storm, his demand for obedience from his crew—he had a tender side to his nature that he showed me on rare occasions. He never trusted his own judgment in giving me advice. Every time I went to him with a question about life that puzzled my young mind he would turn to his old worn Bible and quote me a passage that satisfied my questioning.

When I confronted him with a bewildered question about the process of maturity, Father without a word, reached for his Bible. He turned its pages until he found a certain chapter in the Old Testament.

"Joan, listen to this passage. It will tell you better than I can what you should know. If only there was a woman on board, she could tell you better."

Of course I then asked questions and he explained the meaning of the verse. In simple words Father revealed to me the mysteries of maturity. To me it was so beautiful that I pitied the sailors because they were not the chosen ones of God.

From that time on everything in Nature took on a different meaning to me. Ashore on the islands I sought out native women to play with. I was afraid to ask them questions but I wanted to watch them to see if I was just as they were. One day, on a little island about eighty miles south of Suva, I went ashore with four of our crew and Stitches to get some breadfruit and guavas. We took a sack of nails and rope to use as commodities of trade. Once ashore, Stitches and I left the sailors and wandered through the village streets. We hadn't gone more than a quarter of a mile before we were attracted to a group of natives playing tom-toms. We pushed through the outer circle of natives to see what was happening. There in the center of the group I saw a native mother in child-birth. Unaided by any other woman, when her time came, she squatted on the sand. The tom-toms were being played in celebration of a child's being born to their tribe. Just at the moment the baby came from the mother the natives broke into an ecstatic song of triumph. Apparently paying no attention to her audience, the native mother broke the navel cord that bound the infant to her and tied the end of it with a piece of coconut fiber. Then she took her baby down to the surf and washed it in the cold sea water which brought its first cry of life. The natives lost interest in her as soon as they heard the baby's tiny voice, and they scattered, leaving her to her task of nurturing the little life.

"Your Old Man will get sore if he finds out I'm letting you watch this, Skipper," observed Stitches. "But there's no telling when you'll ever see the likes of this again."

I didn't care what happened to me afterwards for I was so fascinated with the native mother that I didn't want to leave her. She put the baby to her breast to suckle it. After it had its first meal she scraped a place in the sand under the warm sun for it to sleep in, then she lay beside it, full of pride and content. I thought it must be fun to have a baby and have a lot of natives singing and dancing to celebrate the event, but I was to learn years later that most civilized women didn't agree with me.

When we returned to the ship I was full of my latest experience. But somehow life had turned from a simple thing into something so full of puzzling contradictions that I longed to leave the ship and live on shore where I thought I would find an answer to everything that bewildered me.

Within a year from that time I found out that sailors' loves were not all beautiful. They talked of the women on the waterfront they gave their pay to for a night's love; they remembered young sweethearts in the Old Country; and I heard them say they were sweet on the little native girls. But their affairs were confused in my mind. One day I asked Swede, while he was standing at the helm, if he had ever been in love.

"Sure, Skipper, all us sailormen are in love—with the same woman!"

"How do you mean, Swede?" I queried.

"Yep, the same woman satisfies us all. You know how the sails look at night, filled out in firm curves by the wind?"

"Yes," I answered, but I failed to see the connection of sails with Swede's sweetheart.

"Well," he went on, "them sails are so pretty and round, that with the moon lighting them up they looks like a woman's breasts and us sailormen stand aft at the helm just content to follow them wherever they lead."

"I like the water better than sails, Swede," I offered. "When I swim in the sea, with the waves lapping at my body, it feels like millions of little mouths were kissing me."

Swede didn't answer me, but he nearly swallowed his wad of tobacco in his astonishment. I decided not to tell him any more of my secrets if he was going to get so scared of them. That night I turned in my bunk early so that I could think of love. Just thinking about it made me feel funny, as if I was hungry and yet I wasn't hungry. I woke up from a sound sleep feeling cold all over but my face was burning hot. The next morning I made up my mind I wasn't going to think about love any more because it frightened me.

The first disillusion about sex came to me when the Chief of the little island we had visited south of Suva refused to let us land again.

The Chief felt to his tribe as a father feels to his family. There was bitterness in his voice, where a scant year before he had welcomed us.

"Last trip here, some your sailors bring sickness to my people. Many maidens die quickly. I cannot let your white man come on this island ever again."

"How do you know it was some of my men?" Father asked the Chief.

"After white man make love, maidens get sick. One get so sick she throw herself in the sea."

I loved the natives but I was more loyal to our crew.

"How the hell could any one of our crew hurt the native girls?" I demanded.

The Chief ignored me. His quarrel was with the white Chief, my father, and I had no place in the conversation. But after the Chief left, I sought out Father.

"What did the Chief mean about our sailors?" I asked. Father tried to explain to me that one or two of our men were sick—sick with something that was like living death and they had given that sickness to two native girls. The malady spread rapidly because the natives are so in-bred that their resistance is not strong enough to throw off disease. When the full purport of Father's explanation came to me I experienced my first hate and intolerance of men. It wasn't that I cared what the sailors did, but I resented their conduct keeping me from going ashore and being welcomed.

Father saw the hate in my eyes as I listened to him. Once more he fell back upon his Bible to explain to my child mind a problem too complex for his tongue. He read to me the parable of the Adulteress and then he attempted to explain it.

"The greatest Philosopher among men understood sex; it is in everyone's life and in promiscuity alone is there evil. He was pretty wise, Joan, and He understood. Understandin' is greater than forgiveness!" Such was the wise interpretation Father put on the parable to comfort me. I don't think he realized that he had given me the great gift of tolerance.—Though I could understand I couldn't get over the hate within me—Father watched me silently for a while and then spoke:—

"You shouldn't be hatin' anything, Joan," he said,

hatin's like a headwind—it won't get you nowhere."

"Didn't you ever in your life hate anything?" I asked him.

My question landed home to him. Father started to answer No—then he paused and looking beyond me as if seeing his past, he said, bitterly:

"It's the biggest mistake I ever made, Joan—carryin' a festerin' hate in my heart for fourteen years—hate of them that wrecked my ship and killed my men."

Then, with a break in his voice he told me the story of the famous wreck of the *Star*. Father made me promise never to repeat it, for he wanted its memory lost forever. I would never have told it as long as he lived for his sake, but he is still alive, and when I wrote to him that I was going to write *The Cradle of the Deep* he sent me the following letter:

My Dear Joan:

I take my pen in hand to reply to your letter advising me that you are going to write a story of your early life at sea with your old Daddy. There is something I wish you would write of—the story of the wreck of my old full-rigged ship *Star*.

If it hadn't been for that wreck I would never have steered my course South to the Southern Cross and the Atoll Islands of the Pacific. I loved the North, the Aurora Borealis and the magnificent splendor of the icebound Arctic. I knew it as you know your navigation. It I hadn't left it you would never have lived in the tropics and thrived on coconut milk and yarrow root. Instead you might have chawed blubber with the Eskimos.

I would prefer to let sleeping dogs lie, for the memory of that wreck is a bitter one for me, but I want you to tell it anyway so that the world may have a glimpse into the realism of the sea in fact.

Keep a strong hand on the helm and watch for squalls from leeward.

Your affectionate

FATHER.

II

"The Sea gives up its dead"

SAN FRANCISCO in April. High out of the network of masts and rigging of ships that made the waterfront look like a black spider web across the skyline, jerked the blue house flag, with its flying fish tails, of the famous *Star,* queen of the fleet of sailing ships in the Alaska salmon trade. The American flag fluttered no less proudly from her spanker gaff. It was Spring and sailing day!

The *Star* was making ready to sail for Wrangel, Alaska. On board the crew, canners and fishermen, one hundred and thirty-eight in all, eagerly awaited the start. It was a strange conglomeration of humans gathered from the ends of the earth. Quartered in the forward hold the Chinese canners disputed the space with thousands of bitterly resentful rats. A Chinese cook prepared their native food for the canners, and over the crowded hold, filled with squealing rats and chattering Chinese, a brass Joss god, made fast to an under beam, looked calmly down. Him the Chinese worshipped believing he would bring them good luck. What the rats thought about the brass Joss no one knew or cared. Probably they respected him for he was the only thing in the hold they could not bite successfully!

The crew of all nations, Swedes, Yankees, Chinese, Irish, lived in the fo'c's'le head.

Amidships was a veritable little Italy. The Italian fishermen were housed in cabins on deck. They too carried their native Italian cook who prepared rich-smelling Italian foods. The aromas of their cooking, when wafted forward and merged with the smell of boiling rice and herbs from the Chinese hold, made a queer combination of Latin and Oriental odors.

Then, maintaining the peculiar social distinctions of the sea, the white tradesmen and officers of the ship and cannery lived aft in luxurious quarters. The walls of the cabins were of bird's eye maple. In the dining salon hung a six foot oil painting of the *Star* under full sail outriding a hurricane. The swinging lamps were brass, ornately decorated with whales' teeth and carved ivories. In my father's cabin, curtains of red plush proclaimed the captain's aloofness. A "telltale" compass over his bunk and a rack of rifles within easy reach were additional furnishings.

On April 8th, my father stood at the taffrail watching the finishing of the loading of great pieces of steel machinery for the cannery, barrels of oils and salt, and lumber to rebuild some of the warehouses of the company in far distant Wrangel. At his side stood my mother, fighting back, as she had done every year for fifteen years, the quiver of sorrow that sailing day always brought her.

Father would be gone for six months. He would sail up past Nome into the frozen Arctic, and if luck was with him, sail back the following fall before the ice froze him in.

Father looked at her with a twinkle in his eye.

"What's the matter, Mother?"

"Nothing," she answered, "only I wish Joan was old enough so that I could go with you this trip. I feel you are in danger." She forced a smile she was far from feeling. A deadly foreboding that seems to be instinctive with the womenfolk of deep sea sailors came upon her.

"Shame on you, Mother. Why I'll outsail the *Star of Alaska* and the *Star of Nome* and the *Star of the North* by a month. Don't let the crew see you weakening." The mate interrupted them:

"Beg pardon, sir. It's time to let the men knock off for lunch and their last mug of beer. It always makes them sail happier if they have an hour on sailing day to get drunk and kiss their sweethearts good-bye."

"Let them knock off now and come back at four o'clock," instructed Father, "I was a young fellow myself once."

No sooner had the men left their stations on the deck and were ashore than a ripping, tearing roar brought Father rushing to the poop deck. The main yard had broken from the spar and had crashed through the rigging down to the deck as if cut by an invisible hand! It broke into three pieces, but miraculously injured no one. That ill omen was to be remembered later. A mast breaking in three pieces is a sign that before the trip is completed the vessel itself will break into as many parts. Folk laugh at the superstitions of sailormen, but few who have lived at sea will dispute their justification.

Instead of sailing, the *Star* went back to the drydock where the new yard was rigged on. It took three days, and on April 11th, at the five o'clock flood tide, the *Star* was once more ready to go. The crowd jostled on the docks. Chinese women in their quaint native costumes of pants and jackets stood on the wharf near the fo'c's'le head, their waxen faces immobile beneath their shining black hair ornamented with jades and corals. The Italian women were most demonstrative. Their shawls were torn from their heads as they jumbled against each other, pushing for the extreme edge of the dock. Tears and laughter fought for supremacy as they waved good-bye to the Italian fishermen amidships. One young wife with two babies tugging at her skirts was praying, and here and there a rosary was thrust into the hands of the departing fishermen. The American friends of the officers and traders were on the dock nearest the stern, and handkerchiefs and jokes of bravado sent the *Star* off to the Arctic.

My father stood at the helm and with a bellow ordered, "Let go the hawsers!"

"Let go the hawsers," echoed back at him from the fo'c's'le head, and the cobra-like ropes that held the *Star* to her mooring splashed limp into the bay as the men hauled in their slack on the capstan to the accompaniment of a chantey. The Chinese on board set off thousands of firecrackers to foil off the devil, and threw countless red streamers into the air. The Italians sang and gesticulated with their arms as the tug *Dundee* pulled the *Star* out into the harbor. My father is a registered pilot of San Francisco harbor, so he directed the course of the *Star* as they set her sails just off Alcatraz Island, and sailed majestically out of the Golden Gate and nosed her way north.

A quick trip of twenty-seven days brought the *Star* to Wrangel. In five months her mission was completed. She was loaded with fifty-four thousand cases of fine Alaska salmon to take back to San Francisco. It was a dull, thick daybreak as the tugs steamed alongside. All hands were aboard, glad their hard work was done, and jubilant at being homeward bound. The last to come down to the ship was my father. As he walked down the dock, little Arvis Babler, the nine year old daughter of the cannery superintendent, ran along beside him holding his hand. She chattered gaily about his ship. She even suggested that some day he would bring his little girl to Alaska to play with her. None of her light spirit infected my father. He only stared gloomily and silently at the loaded vessel.

"What's the matter, Captain?" she asked, when Father didn't respond to her. "I should think you would be happy today when you are going home."

"I feel as if I were going to my grave," he answered.

The tugs *Hattie H.* and *Kyak* were to tow the *Star* out. Nearly all the crew of these two tugs were drunk before they left the dock. In that alone they violated the code of the sea, but in Alaska at that time there was but one tugboat company and no competition to make a high standard of seamanship necessary. To make matters worse, the rival captains of the two tugs were fighting over which was to be the leading boat. Finally they settled their dispute, apparently to the satisfaction of neither, and the tugs started to pull the *Star* down the Wrangel Narrows, a distance of one hundred and twenty-five miles to the sea. In that dangerous passage there was only room for one ship to pass. At the mouth of the Narrows the *Star* was to set her sails and steer a course off shore for home. All day long the tugs towed her slowly. Meantime those on board the leading tug had celebrated their victory over the crew of the rival tug so thoroughly that the boat was left in charge of a boy mate—while the engineer, to put it mildly, was far from at his best.

Toward night the sky became overcast and the wind increased with the coming darkness. By eight o'clock a gale had arisen. It was off Coronation Island that my father noticed that the tugs were dragging his ship over to the north or dangerous side of the channel. He could hear, above the moaning of the gale, breakers crashing on the rocks! Father tried to signal the tugs of the danger, for their crews evidently had not realized it. Vainly he called through his megaphone, and vainly he sent up flares to attract the attention of the captain of the first tugboat. The condition of the men on those tugs must have kept them from recognizing the warning calls for they pulled on and on towards the shore in the face of the rising gale. Finally at the tugboat end of the forward hawser, some deck hand on the *Hattie H.* saw the cable slacken. They had towed the *Star* into a dangerous bight or indenture in the cliffs. Panic-stricken, the *Hattie H.* pulled off to one side leaving the *Star* in a straddled position between the two tugs. Neither tug was very powerful, but together and properly handled they could have dragged the ship out of danger. Instead the tugs see-sawed against each other doing nothing. Apparently those supposed to be in command did not know what to do.

Nearer and nearer the treacherous rocks the *Star* was

driven by the wind. In desperation Father dropped both anchors to hold her. No sooner had he dropped the anchors than the tugboats, instead of fighting for the ship and the lives of the men on board, cut their towing hawsers and ran for it—deliberately steaming away at full speed, presumably for Wrangel. They didn't even heave to long enough to see what the *Star's* fate was. Later the master of the *Hattie H.* said he thought the *Star* was pounding to pieces on the rocks. (He had heard the anchor chain running out of the hawse pipe!) The *Kyak* steamed to shelter in the lee of an adjacent island. The *Hattie H.* returned to Wrangel, arriving the following Sunday morning. Her master, after the disaster, was asked why he did not stand by to assist the ship.

"What the hell could I do? She was wrecked anyway," he went on record as saying. But had those tugs stood by what followed would never have happened.

On the *Star* the crew huddled on deck all night through, listening to the menacing hissing of the hidden surf crashing against the rocky cliffs. Would the anchors hold? That was fate—there was nothing they could do.

Dawn brought no hope. Scarce five hundred yards off loomed precipitous cliffs with huge waves dashing against them.

Only the anchors still held. If they should slip! But the men fought back that picture of inevitable destruction. Those tugs were surely coming back! They had only disappeared in the night to go for help! Waiting was torture. If only the tugs came back in time.

Hours passed. No tugs appeared. Then the anchors began to slip. The terrific strain of the huge waves was too great for the hooks to hold. Hours on hours! Waiting was gruesome now, as the anchors dragged and the men on board watched the jagged-toothed rocks come nearer. The heavy load of salmon in the holds shifted, and the *Star* listed first to starboard and then to port as each ground swell that rose lifted her high and carried her nearer the barren cliffs.

Father gave instructions to the men to make preparations for getting ashore when the ship struck. Life preservers were fastened on the Chinese who had become panic-stricken. The white officers and officials of the cannery company, realizing the added danger of a hundred crazed Chinese rioting, begged my father to batten them down in the hold like so much cattle to keep them off the decks. Father called the Boss Chinaman to him.

"Boss, you guarantee that your men not riot?" he began. "I won't lock them down in hold. You tell them if danger come Captain tell you."

That old Boss Chinaman had been with Father for fourteen years and he trusted him almost as he trusted his Joss god. He went back to his Chinamen in the hold and told them of my father's promise, and they were calmed to a degree. They cramped together in their hold paralyzed with fear, but they kept off the decks.

After Father had seen to the Chinamen and Italian fishermen, he returned aft to the officers' quarters and told them to be prepared for the worst as the anchors were useless now. Down in the stuffy red plush cabin the men sat around the chart table. They were all silent and depressed. They all had a look of finality on their faces. It was small choice—on deck they could see sure death looming up; in the cabin they could shut their eyes to it and wait! In the last few moments of their lives strange reactions took place in them. The clerk of the cannery, a man about thirty-three years of age, pale and husky-voiced, asked my father to take the money he had, nine hundred dollars, and give it to his family, when my father reached San Francisco. Another man asked Father to take a message to his wife, and still another broke out into vile profanity. A huge man, one of the wealthy owners of the cannery, forgot his pose of dignity and knelt down on the cabin floor and prayed like a frightened child.

"You all have the same chances, men, and each one of you will bear your own responsibility," Father told them in answer to their pleas.

He set about to have a trunk packed with medicines and stimulants which was taken on deck. Later that trunk was picked up in the wreckage ashore and the contents helped revive some of the men and dress their injuries. Only four lived of the white men who sat around the table in the cabin awaiting the verdict of the storm.

On deck the flying spray from the mountainous seas was like a white blinding screen, but Father could see Ole Swenson, a Norse man, powerful and gigantic, standing on the fo'c's'le head scanning the horizon for the return of the tugs. Swenson saw nothing but the storm rising in velocity, and the cliffs looming blacker on shore. Roaring and cursing against the fate that was murdering his beloved ship, Ole Swenson jumped into the sea to end his agony.

It was only a matter of minutes before sure death would claim the hundred and thirty-eight men on the *Star*. Father called for volunteers to man a boat and take a line ashore so that a breeches buoy could be rigged. A breeches buoy is a little buoy on a rope, made fast to the mast and on some point on shore, much like a big pulley line, by which shipwrecked men can slide to the mainland high above a pounding surf. Four young men responded to his call for volunteers. Among them were two brothers, Hasen by name. One of them, the younger, couldn't swim. His older brother urged him not to go. He, the older one would go, for he was a strong swimmer. The younger boy would not hear his pleading and went first. The good swimmer was drowned just out of reach of help a few moments later.

With great difficulty the crew swung a lifeboat off its davits with the four young men in it fighting for their lives against the running sea. The men on the *Star* watched them pull for the shore—watched them almost get in—and then saw their shell of a boat dashed on the rocks of the narrow beach. Three of them jumped to safety and were cheered by the crew on board whose lives they would save.

The three men dragged the rope up and fastened it on a tree trunk high out of reach of the waves. This done, they turned their attention to fastening the running rope which would propel the breeches buoy, but that line had broken loose and was lost in the sea. Father called for another volunteer to go ashore with another line to replace it. The ship's carpenter stepped forward. He tied the rope to his body and ascended the rigging, then hand over hand he slid along the rope which the men had stretched to the shore. The *Star* was toppling like a drunken sailor from side to side. The men on board watched the carpenter get caught in a green comber which first sucked him under and then threw him high

in the air. When he was almost ashore an extra hard
strain flipped him off like a fly from a rubber band. He
struck the water with a terrific blow on his back. He was
close enough to shore for the three surviving young men
to pull him in to safety.

Then the end came! The *Star* crashed on the saw-
toothed rocks. The forward part of her, the fo'c's'le head
and the foremast broke off just before the crew fled aft.
They hung on like leeches to the after railing and deck
houses. The force of the relentless pounding sea was so
great that the *Star* quivered and broke into three pieces,
just as her yard arm had broken on that ominous day in
San Francisco. The stern of the ship was all that was
afloat and that was covered by screaming, frightened men.
The sea around was a seething mass of salmon cases, dead
Chinamen, screaming Italians and Americans being
smothered in the spray. The waves licked up viciously
as if to devour the few hanging on for life on the stern.
Clinging to the wheelhouse and after railing, a small
group of officials and white men held their balance. A sea
lifted a piece of wreckage to windward as if to capsize
it and most of the men jumped in the opposite direction
to avoid being pinned beneath. Three remained with my
father. The piece of wreckage, instead of turning turtle
to windward, was caught in the backwash of a wave and
capsized with all remaining hands to leeward! They
came up into a seething maelstrom of pitching wreckage,
packing-cases swirling, outstretched arms and kicking
legs of drowning men, shrieks of fear and the terrible seas
breaking with a roar over all. And on the shore, only
two hundred yards away, four of the five men who had
taken the first desperate chances, waited helpless. They

scanned the incoming combers for bodies, Chinese or white, that might wash in close enough to fish out, but the shore was abrupt and it had become piled with the cargo and wreckage from the *Star*. The men could reach only a few and yank them out of the jaws of the sea as they washed in.

When the last man had left the wreck my father jumped overboard. He said it took about a half a minute for him to reach the surface. He felt a heavy bulk above his head when he was under the water. He thought it was the keel of his ship and that he was pinned beneath it. Holding his breath, he made one herculean effort to rise to the surface. The "bulk" over his head was the top of one of the hatchings which had broken loose from the ship and was floating on the sea. Father struck out for the shore. The icy water numbed his senses. He remembered nothing more. A big green roller crested with salmon cases overtook him and one of them struck him on the head and mercifully knocked him unconscious. The backwash of the surf carried his inert body to the beach.

Of the one hundred and thirty-eight men on board, only twenty-seven survived. Those that reached the shore before my father set about to rescue the others. Two of them, the carpenter and a Scotch sailor named Frank Muir, pulled my father's body out of the water.

"The Old Man's drowned. Let's pull out the living ones," spoke up the carpenter and he went down the beach to salvage more of the men. Frank Muir was as devoted to my father as a son. He didn't heed the carpenter, but dragged the apparently dead body to the shelter of a rock and tried to revive him. It seemed a thankless task. The Captain was gone. If he couldn't save him he would at least bury him away from the others, and Frank Muir carried Father higher up to a little table of rock in the cliff. There he rolled him and pounded him until a glow of life came into his battered, frozen body.

By late afternoon no life could be seen in the surf. My father was so crippled and frozen that he couldn't walk. He crawled around on all fours directing his men in reviving the others. No rest for any until, beyond any doubt, all were rescued that it was possible to rescue.

"We won't give up until we find all of us," said my father, and the twenty-seven survivors agreed to a man.

They set about to search the wreckage that was piled high on the beach for bodies. They found several groups of men, dead men, so entangled and twisted together by the churning of the sea that they couldn't be pulled apart. Dismembered bodies were strewn on the rocky coast like driftwood. Arms and legs and headless trunks washed back and forth in the foam. One living being was found in the mess, a Japanese. He was buried in a hill of salmon cases. The men had to burrow to get into it. He was very weak through loss of blood from a gash extending from his temple the length of his chin!

By dragging wreckage together the men built a huge fire around which they snuggled for warmth. Instead of relief the fire was only an added torture, a Dante's Inferno, for the thick smoke from the damp wood blinded them.

In the morning the bodies of the white men were gathered, and shallow graves dug for them in the rocky shore to keep the wolves from eating them. Over the graves Father ordered the men to pile heavy debris so that the sea washing up couldn't snatch them back to a watery grave.

The lot of the survivors was almost as bad as that of the lost men, for there was no sign of rescue, and the coast was barren of habitation for hundreds of miles around. The icy wind made existence almost impossible.

The next day one of the tugs returned. Her captain was surprised to see the men ashore for he had not dreamed that supposedly dead men could live to tell the tale. It was too rough to send a boat in, but the tug hove to until the following day, when the crew took aboard the survivors and returned to Wrangel. The survivors were so incensed against the tug crew for cutting the hawser and sending one hundred and eleven men to their death that they started to murder them. Father stopped the violence. He said the law would deal with the tug people when the facts were made known. At Wrangel the survivors were furnished clothing from the cannery store and sent by steamers to San Francisco.

Several days after the wreck, the company's tugs were sent with a crew to dispose of the bodies on Coronation Island. They found an indescribable confusion of corpses, provisions and debris covering the shore for a depth of many feet. Pieces of human bodies were mingled with the sides of hams and bacons and canned goods which the sea spewed up from the ship's holds. Instead of segregating the bodies, the rescue crew drove picks into them and dragged them into heaps. After they had made piles of human wreckage they poured oil over them and set them afire like so much rubbish. Then they did something that is almost beyond human comprehension. After they had burned the bodies, they salvaged the hams and bacons and other foods they found mixed with the dead men and took them back to Wrangel where they sold them to the Eskimos.

What became of the few survivors? They were scattered by the company that owned the tugboats so that they couldn't be used to witness against them. Those whose injuries prevented employment were treated in hospitals—the others were placed on various ships.

My mother was in San Francisco waiting for any bit of news of the survivors. The report came to her that my father's dead body had been found, mangled almost beyond recognition, and then the report was confirmed. I was only six months old at the time. The shock to my mother brought her an illness from which she has never recovered. It was through this illness that I came to be raised by my father.

Father was retained on full salary during the official investigation of the wreck. Then he learned how much law, justice or right mean to greedy and selfish men. The tugs belonged to the same company that owned the *Star*. If the responsibility for the wreck was fastened on the two captains of the tugboats, the corporation faced enormous damage suits from the families and dependents of the hundred and eleven dead men. So the owners used every bit of their influence and resources to protect the guilty tugboat captains. The verdict acquitted them— the blame rested on the gale! And thus they settled the most famous and most unnecessary wreck in American maritime history. My father was fired in disgrace with the remark: "We have no ship for you now."

That was the way he was rewarded for his effort to

procure the "justice" he had promised his men when they wanted to avenge the murder done by the crews of the tugboats. The slogan went from Alaska to Seattle after the verdict: "Don't kick Power."

Fifteen years of faithful and intelligent service in the Arctic swept away in a night! Father could never go North again. The bodies of a hundred and eleven men on the rocks of Coronation Island would drive him to murder. He bought an old schooner and turned to the opposite end of the world, the South Seas, warmth and maybe forgetfulness!—But he still carries the bitterness and hate in his heart!

12

A cursing contest and a hangman's noose

MOST of the men I knew were typical old shellback sailors, a species of human that began to go out with the increase of steam vessels until now the type is almost extinct. The shellback was unlike any other human, a law unto himself, with few wants and a large philosophy of content that was none the less real because he grumbled all the time. His ration of tobacco, enough money for grog, and a few days in port at the end of a long sea trip to blow his pay on some skirt, satisfied his creature desires. For mental relaxation he cursed the ship, cursed his officers, cursed the grub and cursed the cook, and withal, he wouldn't have traded places with any king on his throne.

The shellback's attitude toward the sea was all his own, and quite typical of the breed. He loved it—he lived on it. He expected to be on top of the waves all his life and beneath them when he died. And so fatalistic was he, that half of the deep sea sailors never learned to swim! Stitches expressed the attitude best.

"What's the use of learnin' to swim?" he argued. "Any sailor dumb enough to fall overboard oughta drown and if he's washed overboard he couldn't swim anyhow—so what's the use?"

"But Father made me learn to swim," I protested.

"That's different," grinned Stitches. "You see, Skipper, the Captain knows a woman ain't got sense enough not to fall overboard. Now if you was to fall overboard and couldn't swim, some dumb sailor, whether he could swim or not, would jump in and get drowned trying to save you; but bein' as you kin swim, if *you* fall overboard, nobody don't worry—they just toss you a rope and you pull out by yourself and the Captain don't lose no good sailor. All that happens is you come back aboard and you get your stern tanned with a rope's end to warm up the chill. No ma'am! Captain ain't goin' to let no good sailor go dead tryin' to save a woman."

Quite unconvinced, I puzzled and puzzled over Stitches' point of view, but it was not until some years later, in one tragic moment, that I learned how wide can be the difference between a man's philosophy and his action in a crisis.

Next to Stitches the most interesting shellback I ever knew was John Henry, a withered old seaman close to seventy, with a cracked whiskey voice and a face so furrowed that it looked like the relief map of a mountain range. He chawed a hunk of tobacco incessantly and the juice drooled down his chin, leaving a little yellow rut marked in his whiskers. He had sailed the Horn a hundred times, to hear him tell it, and he would have been a captain long ago instead of a common seaman, only a captain couldn't get drunk in public on the waterfront—so John Henry preferred not to be a captain. But for all his shortcomings, John Henry was a real seaman. An ordinary gale was music to his soul and a hurricane seemed to take off thirty years—for no young man could hold to the foot ropes aloft better than he and few could steer a dangerous course as well.

We shipped John Henry at Frisco and in a week Stitches' nose was out of joint, for John Henry had quite won me. He would sit for hours, on his watch below, and teach me to tie intricate sailor knots—everything from splices, monkey fists, running bowlines, Turk's heads, true lover's knots to a hangman's noose.

"I bin in every jail from Seattle to Port Said," he confided, "an' I can learn you every kind of a knot they use for killin' off undesirables."

Stitches was disgusted.

"Damned old shellback! Teaching you how to tie knots to get rid of undesirables, is he? I dunno nobody as undesirable as he is. If he had what was comin' to him, somebody'd tie a knot for him long ago. Mebbe they will yet."

On the end of a halyard John Henry was chief chanteyman. One day I was helping haul in the slack of the fore topsail and he said:

"You gotta eat more beans before you can pull like a regular sailor. Women ain't no use on a ship except to eat up grub."

Then he burst into a chantey that sailors sing about "Womenfolk on Ships," and put my name in it.

This is the song:

"Sweet Joan, a maiden of fourteen years old,
    Not once in her life had been kissed.
    Except by her cats and her dogs, I been told,
    And the beauties of life she had missed.

"And OH! how she longed for the love of a man
    But all seemed to turn her away.
    Till one day she set on a capital plan
    And put it in form this way.

"Now sailors are jolly good fellows, thought she,
    To take a trip she'd a notion,
    For sailors oft get very blue out at sea,
    And—girls are scarce on the ocean!"

"Aw, what the hell do you mean by that?" I asked. "I can do something that nobody in the fo'c's'le can do and that is, I can navigate. Father's taught me how to find our position by the Southern Cross at night," I boasted.

"Yeh? Well, I still says women ain't got no place on shipboard. Why, they can't even talk like sailors," and he spat a juicy stream with unerring accuracy through the hawse hole on the port side of the ship.

He had thrown down the challenge to me to make good as a sailor. I was no frail little Captain's daughter that the sailors slew each other to get. I had to win them! From that day on I never lost an opportunity to emulate a deep sea sailor in every way.

At night in my cabin I rubbed my hands over rough rope to make callouses. I began to practise every swear word I heard the sailors use. After a month of careful observation I was able to curse four minutes in succession and never repeat a word. When I had them all down glibly I waylaid John Henry.

"Listen, you bastard," I started, and then I traced his ancestors from several kinds of animals down to biological defects in himself and compared him with every known form of low life and waste products imaginable. When I finished my four minute tirade I stood on guard, thinking he would make a pass at me. Instead he listened intently, then his face broke into a grin:

"You're improvin', Skipper," he complimented me. I was so elated at winning his approval that I thought I would try my vocabulary out on my father. I went up on the poop deck where Father was sitting, smoking his pipe.

"Tell me to do something," I invited him.

"Now, what are you up to?" he asked suspiciously.

"Just you tell me to do something as if I was a sailor in the fo'c's'le," I repeated.

"All right," he replied, pleased at what appeared to be my desire to work. "You get a chip-hammer and chip the rust off the anchor chains. They got to be given a coat of red lead to keep them from rusting away."

Then I let fly with my newly acquired sea language. I got as far as one half minute of it when I felt myself going through space toward the cabin below with my father attached to my collar and the seat of my pants.

"Where in the so and so did you hear any such language as that?" he shouted.

"From you when you're tacking ship and the wind won't catch the sails," I answered, wishing I had never learned them.

"I'll be goddamned if you ever heard your father curse," he yelled. "I'll break your damned neck if I ever hear you curse again—do you hear?"

I heard him. The whole ship heard him with glee. Stitches said he embarrassed the flying fish! Father went on:

"Your mouth ain't fit to put grub in after such language," he roared, "so you don't get no meals until you forget every curse word you know!" and with that he tied a rag over my mouth and went after a piece of rope to warm my posterior.

I was in my bunk, my mouth tied up and my behind too sore to sit on. What I thought of John Henry was worse than the words I had memorized to impress him. I'd get even with him if I died in the attempt. Lying down there on my stomach I couldn't understand where the justice of it came in. I had tried to be a regular sailor and had got the worst of it. However, I was far from licked—I mean in spirit.

I amused myself by watching some bedbugs parading on my straw mattress. Then they gave me an idea. I caught a few and put them on me. At least I could be lousy, and so that much nearer to perfection as a seaman!

At twenty minutes past five the cabin-boy rang the supper bell. I was hungry, but I didn't dare to leave my cabin. I stuck my head out of my porthole and watched the foam making pictures on the water. From experience I knew that was the easiest and surest way to make myself sleepy. Next morning I awoke, ravenously hungry and oh, how repentant my empty insides made me!

I found Father behind a rapidly disappearing bowl of oatmeal in the dining saloon.

"Hey, I'll never curse any more if I can eat," I promised him. He grunted his forgiveness, then added:

"We'll be in Brisbane along about noon today. Don't you dare leave the ship."

"Can't I be the watchman in port and save you the wages?" I inquired, eager to get back in his good graces again.

"That wouldn't be such a bad idea. I don't want none of the crew ashore in this port. I'll have to bail them out of jail for drunkenness, and I haven't got the time nor the money to do that."

"I won't let any of them get away," I assured him.

At about two o'clock we pulled into the harbor after sailing up the long Brisbane River. The Customs officials came aboard and sealed up our stores and tobacco. Then came the port doctors to examine the crew.

"Have the crew strip and line up on deck for examinations, Captain," instructed one of the doctors. "Everyone of them has to be vaccinated before you can land here. We've got some smallpox ashore started by sailors off a ship from China and the Philippines and the harbor is under quarantine."

I hurried down to the main deck to take my place in the line-up of the crew. I was the last in the line. The doctor looked at me curiously, and then said,

"Well, well, little one, if you aren't the very picture of health," and he pinched my muscles, admiringly.

"No, I'm not," I assured him, "I have had everything that sailors have, worse than they get it. You better vaccinate me good," I advised. "I even have bedbugs on me."

That doctor looked horrified, but he dug into my arm with three long scratches even deeper than the men's. It hurt like the devil, but I was very proud at that moment because I had as many as John Henry and just as deep. To this day I carry those scars—proud proof of my equality with sailors.

Before Father went ashore with the Customs officials he admonished me again to let no sailor have shore leave.

"The mate will be busy discharging cargo, and I may not be back before late tonight, so you keep your eye on the gangway."

I took up my station at the gangway and chawed on some dried prunes. They were as close to seamen's tobacco as I dared attempt. The cabin-boy tried to go ashore, but I pushed him back. One or two of the sailors made a bluff at sneaking past but I stood in the middle of the gangway with a belaying pin and forgetting Father's lesson, I laid down the law in language to make John Henry proud. Each time they retired, defeated, but chuckling.

I was hot in the sun, but I didn't care. Proudly I stood my post until six o'clock, when the crew knocked off discharging. Then came the supper bell, and of course, no one could expect me to stay on guard at grub time. In my father's absence I sat in his place opposite the two mates. After I had finished my meal I picked my teeth with a fork just as I had watched the second mate do so many times before. I wouldn't have dared to do that with Father present.

I strolled up on deck to take up my gangway watch again. If any sailor got ashore it would be over my dead body, I promised myself. I sat there for fully two hours.

There was no sign of life from the fo'c's'le. Not one man came out to cross that gangway and go ashore.

"Huh!" I gloated to myself, "they're afraid of me.

They know they can't get away with anything with me here watching."

I was so full of my own sense of importance and authority that I didn't suspect anything queer in the silence forward, until the cabin-boy came aft, after taking the dinner basket back to the galley.

"All them guys forrard is ashore and I'm going to go ashore too," he sniffed at me contemptuously.

"What?" I asked, too surprised to believe I had heard him aright.

"Sure, they all went ashore while you was eating your grub. Nobody left for'ard except the cook."

What could I do? I had gained Father's respect only to lose it when his back was turned. I thought at first I'd go ashore and find the sailors in the saloons and bring them back on board before Father got back. That plan wasn't wise, though, for, if I left, the cabin-boy and the two mates might go ashore in my absence and I would be a complete failure.

I took up the belaying pin and perched myself on the top of the gangway, and waited. I waited until long past midnight before I heard a human sound on the dock. Suddenly my ear caught a thick, throaty song dimly coming from among the cargo piles on the dock:

> "McGinty's back again;
>   He's dressed up like a dandy,
>   He's down at Mike's saloon,
>   He's drinkin' wine and brandy . . ."

It was the voice of John Henry singing the old sailors' funeral dirge "McGinty." McGinty is the legendary sea captain who sank to the bottom of the sea, and when sailors get drunk their favorite vision is of McGinty arisen from the dead and drinking in waterfront saloons.

"John Henry!" I called as loud as I could.

I got no answer, except his drunken voice rising in the old song.

Then he weaved out from the shadow of the cargo piled on the wharf to stand at the foot of the gangway. He was so drunk he could hardly keep his balance. He made three gallant efforts to place his foot on the bottom of the gangway; finally, by grabbing the hand ropes he pulled himself aboard and toppled over on the deck. I lifted him up and shook him violently.

"John Henry, stand up!" I shouted at him.

He babbled something unintelligible and drooled down his shirt front as I shook him. His bloodshot eyes focused on me and held there.

"Get your Ole Man give me money for whiskey. Got to have whiskey."

"You'll get a kick in the seat of the pants, that's what you'll get," I answered him.

"Got to have money for whiskey—only want whiskey," he insisted, and he started to sob pathetically.

"You're drunk, John Henry. Come on and get forrard into your bunk."

He pulled away from me and demanded through his sobs:

"You going to get Ole Man to give me some more money?"

"He isn't here, John Henry. Come on and get forrard and turn in," I coaxed him.

"You get me money for whiskey or I'll croak."

His body began to tremble. His lips were blue, his eyes fiery and bloodshot.

"I don't care if you croak or not," I answered, for I had heard threats like that before.

"All right, gonna croak. You watch me. I'm gonna croak," and he started forward. I followed, hoping to get him safely to his bunk. Just beneath the fo'c's'le head he picked up a long piece of rope that was coiled there on a stanchion.

"See this rope? Gonna croak if you don't get Ole Man get me money, see?" and he burst out crying again. He tied the piece of rope into a hangman's noose, nine slip knots on a loop, just as he had once taught me to tie it months before. He held the noose up to my face and said once more:

"I'll croak if you don't."

Of course I didn't believe him, so I just answered:

"All right, John Henry, you'll feel better when you do!"

Instead of quieting, that seemed to set him off again. He slipped the noose over his head and thrust his face right up against mine.

"Do I get the money?" he half shrieked in his cracked whiskey voice.

Scenes with drunken sailors were no novelty to me. They always made dire threats against themselves, or the captain or their mates, and then they stumbled to bed and forgot it. Now I lost patience.

"You don't get a damned cent," I yelled back at John Henry.

It seemed almost to sober him. He straightened.

"You'll be sorry," he said, and turning with great dignity he marched out of sight forward with the hangman's noose around his neck and the rope trailing on the deck after him.

I turned and with what I conceived to be equal dignity marched back toward the gangway. Duty called me. There would be more drunken sailors to drive to their bunks.

I don't know why I left the gangway after a short ten minutes except that I loved John Henry and felt a vague desire to see that he was all right. But of course I wouldn't let him know that. I couldn't sacrifice my dignity as watchman in charge of the ship. So I marched forward very importantly, past the mizzen, past the mainmast and around the cook's galley and there I found John Henry!

He had tied the rope around the capstan on the fo'c's'le head and jumped down toward the main deck. There he hung, with his feet scarce six inches from the main deck and the hangman's knot under his left ear canting his head rakishly to one side. His body was turning slowly on the rope and as I stared his face came around so his popped eyes stared back at me and his wide opened mouth seemed to sneer, "I told you I'd do it."

Staring into those popped eyes I couldn't cry out—I couldn't move; and then after what seemed a million years the body turned on the rope and the face went away from me, releasing me from my speechless terror. I shrieked, and whirling away I ran aft, down into the lazarette and hid underneath a pile of old canvas. I heard the rats running to safety at my approach to their domains in the dark. I had killed John Henry! I had killed

John Henry! Over and over in a numbing pain the words rushed to my brain!

I don't know exactly how long I stayed there before I heard voices on the deck above me. I was afraid to come out of hiding. I could tell by the excitement that John Henry's body had been found. A few hours before in the afternoon I had been sore at him for encouraging me to curse and now he was dead!

Weak, and still shaking with fright I found my way on deck. I saw Father and a group of strange men on deck surrounding a figure covered with canvas.

I called to Father:

"Here I am. I didn't do it—honest I didn't." And I crumpled over crying.

Father picked me up and held me in his arms.

"What makes you think you did it, Joan?" he asked, so quietly and tenderly that I told him the whole story.

Johnny was buried in Brisbane, but I have never to this day wanted to tie a hangman's noose.

13

Ideas about Women

"WOMEN ain't going to do you no good, Joan. Takin' them by and large they're mostly liars anyhow, and the ones you find around the waterfront is just plain head winds."

We were tied up at the dock in Brisbane, Australia, when Father delivered his dictum. I knew he meant by "women" the gold-toothed, plump barmaids and the laughing sweethearts that swarmed around every arriving ship to get the sailors' pay, or beg curios from them. Those women had always been objects of curiosity to me and Father knew it.

"If any of them women try to talk to you, you go below and don't have anything to do with them, understand?"

I understood and promised to obey. I did not imagine that there was any danger of my not obeying, for two reasons. First, I was afraid of women. Second, they were all much too grand and beautiful ever to pay attention to me. Father had planted that fear of my own sex in me to keep me from picking up with chance women. He was afraid I would learn things from them that would destroy his years of careful protection of my ideals. He never let me look at myself in a mirror.

"You're an ugly kid, Joan, so you won't gain anything from looking at yourself in a mirror."

It would have been worth a sailor's life to offer a mirror to me and in all the years I was on board I don't believe it occurred to any of the men forward. Aft, there was only one looking-glass, a small cracked one used by Father when he shaved in port, and even that he kept carefully hidden from me. My only chance to see myself was in the rain barrels on deck. If you think you can get a good idea of your personal appearance by looking into a rain barrel on a swaying, rolling ship, try it. My face used to ripple back at me like a blurred cabbage. As far as I knew I looked exactly like that image reflected in the rain barrel, so of course I believed Father when he told me I was so ugly that women ashore looking at my face would laugh at me.

Since then Father has confessed he made me think myself hopelessly ugly so that I should never be conceited. He said it was one of his dreams for me that I should be unspoiled and be beautiful inside. But, I did not know that then, and I believed all he said about my personal appearance.

How I used to envy the barmaids and the sweethearts about the docks! To me they seemed so beautiful and the sailors were always so glad to see them. No sailor, save old Stitches, ever seemed really glad to see me. The crew all thought I was a nuisance. Father's warning was unnecessary. I would not have dared to speak to those beautiful land women.

The day after he so put me on my guard I was sitting on the skylight aft, watching the cargo boom dip down in the hold and bring up a rope-net full of copra and swing it over to the dock where the stevedores dumped it into a big dory. McLean and Axel Oleson were on duty at the mizzen hatch where they bellowed orders to the crew below to get the "barnacles off their sterns and load up the nets quicker." The men below seemed in no mood to hurry, judging by Oleson's remarks to them, for he traced their ancestors to dubious origins in English and Scandinavian. It was no novelty to me to hear such talk —it wasn't even varied enough to keep me interested.

I was beginning to get tired of watching when from my perch on the skylight I saw a pretty woman coming down the dock. She walked slowly as if she wasn't sure of her destination, but when she drew close enough to the ship to be noticed she became all smiles. She pretended she didn't see McLean and Axel on deck, but I could tell she did see them by the careful way she avoided looking at them. She came up the gangway, which was just forward of the poop deck and spoke to me.

"Hello, little girl," she said.

I got all goose flesh, I was so thrilled at being noticed. All thought of Father's warning vanished.

"Hello," I answered. "Where the hell are you going? Have you got business on this ship?" I was being very nautical, as it was my one chance to show off my authority.

She was so fluffy and soft-looking, surely she couldn't

hurt me. Now she was staring at me—at my overalls and my bare feet sticking out beneath them.

"You know you're a bloody pretty kid," she said. I flushed to the roots of my hair. It was the first time I had ever been paid a compliment. I studied her face closely to see if she was just making fun of me, but she seemed sincere.

"Aw, hell, I'm not as pretty as you, Miss!" I replied, taking in her high heel buttoned shoes and her hat with flowers and ribbons on it. "And you smell good, too." That vision of loveliness was bathed in cheap perfume, but to me it was divine compared to the stink of the rotten copra being hauled out of the hold.

I had no way of judging women except from the conversation among the sailors that I had caught. I thought every woman's character was measured by her ankles and her hips, for often I had heard the sailors say: "a good pair of hips and little ankles is worth nine months' pay." So, using their standard of perfection of womanhood, I measured the woman who stood before me. She was perfect.

"Got any glad rags, Kid?" she asked.

"No, but I've got some tapa cloth and two tortoise-shell bracelets with pearl in them," I answered, hoping to impress her.

"I mean, haven't you got any pretties to go around with gents? I bet all the sailors aboard here are nuts about you."

"No, they ain't," I answered hastily. "If I ever lay down on the job of pulling on ropes when I'm needed, or get in their way when they unload a cargo, they kick my pants for me."

She became very much interested in me.

"Say, what do you stick on this bloody barge for? You ought to be down with me and the girls where you'd be appreciated."

"You mean leave the ship?"

"Sure, I'll get you a swell job with me and the girls down at the Union Hotel."

It sounded wonderful to me. I was tired of staying on the ship, day after day in port, with no one to play with. Perhaps I would find companions ashore. I was sure no harm could come from just going with her for a little while. For a moment I hesitated, then one glance at her thin ankles and her broad hips assured me that she must be a good woman. Proudly I followed her down the gangway, and as I passed McLean I told him to tell Father I was going to take a job at the Union Hotel for a few days until the ship was ready to sail.

How set up I was to be walking along the dock with this beautiful woman who thought I was pretty!

The Union Hotel was a small, dingy-looking place about a block from the wharf. I had passed it several times on my walks ashore with Father, and I had heard the sailors speak of it as the "Seamen's Rest." They always grinned when they said that and I wondered why.

"Come in and meet my lady friends," urged my new friend. I accompanied her gladly. The stuffy interior of the cheap waterfront hotel seemed the height of elegance to me. We entered the "pub" (English for saloon).

"Where's the job?" I asked, for on shipboard the first thing a man did was to get to work. Then I discovered that my guide and her "lady friends" were barmaids.

"Here, sailor-girl, you take this end station, and you'll

get lots of tips. Sometimes the blokes gives as much as six-
pence if we smile pretty."

I was so pleased to be accepted by those women that I
put my conscience out of its misery about leaving the ship
and went to my station behind the bar. I was having a
lot of fun until some sweating stevedores came in.

"Beer for us," was their order.

One of the group I recognized as the cargo tally man
from our dock. He seemed shocked to see me behind the
bar drawing foamy mugs of beer.

"Say, does your old man know you're here?" he asked
suspiciously.

"It's none of your business," I answered. The girls
giggled and encouraged me to go on. "Besides, I can
knock your block off if you squeal on me." Again the barmaids cheered me on. The other stevedores gathered
around and began guying him, but the tally man persisted:

"I've known your father off and on for fifteen years
and I'm going to take you back on board ship for him."
He reached over and pulled me by the arm to hasten my
departure.

"I'm warning you to take your hands off me or I'll
knock your block off," I snarled at him. I was thrilled at
being the center of attention. I wanted to show off in
front of the barmaids how strong I was and how well I
could scrap. The tally man seemed to have but one
thought—to get me out of the place in a hurry even if he
had to use force to do it. I was equally determined to
stand my ground. He tried to pull me to the door. I
swung around on him and hit him as hard as I could.
The girls cheered me again. I hit the tally man once more,

then he took me by the shoulders and shook me like a rag.

That was too humiliating; I saw red. Hitting, kicking, butting with my head, I sailed into him. Taken by surprise he went down. The barmaids let out squeals of delight—the stevedores roared with laughter. We were on the sawdust floor of the pub, rolling over and over, punching and clawing. He didn't want to hurt me and I wanted to kill him. That made it almost an even fight.

For about three minutes we were at it and then I found myself flat on my face with one of his hands gripping my neck and my own right fist held up between my shoulder blades. It was the hammerlock hold I had seen used in sailor fights and I was completely helpless.

"Now, you little hell-cat, you march back to that ship," he growled, and lifted me from the floor, pushed me out the door, and walked me down the dock to the vessel. I had a cut lip and a black eye. The tally man called to McLean:

"Say, you better watch this kid until her father gets back. She was hanging around a bar down at the Union Hotel—and that joint's a bed house."

I hurried below and washed the blood from my face, ashamed that any of our sailors should see me licked. But no matter how I scrubbed I couldn't erase my black eye so I decided to get in my bunk and not attract Father's attention to me. It seemed I always remembered to obey Father after I had forgotten to!

When Father returned to the ship he came in my cabin and asked:

"What are you turning in so early for?"

I took great care to lie face downwards so he couldn't see my eyes as I told him:

"I don't feel very well. Guess I don't want any supper."

What relief! I could see Father hadn't heard of my humiliating defeat at the hands of a tally man in the Union Hotel.

"If you're sick, there's no use bellyaching about it. I'll fix you up a dose of salts and that'll get the kinks out of you."

He brought me a coffee mug half full of epsom salts. I swallowed the stuff and then I lay there thinking deep and unkind thoughts about women. The laughter of the barmaids as I was marched out of that pub by the tally man still rang in my ears. My soul was bitter within me and I swore to myself that I would never again trust a woman—not even if she smelled of perfume to high heaven and had inch-thin ankles!

But I wasn't to get off from my latest escapade as easily as I had thought. I was still lying in my bunk, trying to figure out how I was fooled by that barmaid, when I heard a man's voice in the companionway asking:

"Can I see the Captain? I gotta tell him something he oughta know."

My heart sank. The voice was that of the tally man and I suspected that he had come to tell on me. I wasn't left in doubt long, for soon I heard Father's indignant voice asking:

"Do you mean to tell me that my kid was in a pub with a barmaid?"

"Yes, Captain, and she started a brawl there. It's pretty dangerous business to leave a girl like her hang around the waterfront. I wouldn't let a kid of mine do it, no sir!"

Their voices dropped to an indistinguishable mumble of words, but I knew the result would be serious. I'd get even with that tally man before he knew it! I'd teach him to squeal on me after he had given me a black eye. Whatever thoughts I had about the matter left me when Father came into my cabin. He wasn't angry, as I expected him to be. Rather he seemed unusually quiet and thoughtful. He sat on the edge of my bunk and after a pause, he said:

"Joan."

"Huh?" I murmured, with my face still hidden in my pillow to hide my telltale black eye.

"Turn over and look at me."

"I know what you look like," I countered, still face downwards. "You haven't changed since I saw you a couple of hours ago."

"Yes, I have changed. I've changed my mind about you." I didn't know what to think about his sudden tack, so I stalled for an opening to defend myself:

"Can't you let a fellow sleep that don't feel good?"

Father took me by the shoulders and turned me over. He didn't say a word about my black eye, he seemed to overlook it.

"Joan, we're going to be here in port about thirty days. I gotta get a new foremast set in, and a general overhaul of the vessel when the cargo is discharged."

I still couldn't see where he was heading.

"You've disobeyed me for the last time. But I'm partly to blame, so I'm not goin' to punish you. Only when you get big enough to go with barmaids and fight with men, it's time to put some thought on your future. I've got a lot of thinkin' to do about you, Joan—a lot of thinkin'."

And he went away leaving me vastly relieved, only had I known what was to come out of his thinking I would have been more worried than ever before in my life.

Father kept me on board ship all during our stay in port, with only occasional walks along the waterfront in his company. We sailed with a cargo of wool and ballast for the United States. We were going to Frisco to get a load of lumber.

After ninety-three days of uneventful sailing we sighted the Farallone Islands off the Golden Gate. A tugboat steamed out thirty miles to pick us up. How excited I was to see the smoke of that tug coming toward us! When it came within hailing distance the captain called through his megaphone:

"Want a tow?"

"How much?" called back Father.

"Four hundred dollars to inside anchorage."

"I'll see you in Hell first," answered Father.

"Two hundred dollars," came back the tugboat captain.

"I'll sail this bloody ship right up to the ferry building under her own canvas," came Father's reply.

Cursing, the tugboat captain let out a string of degrading opinions of the kind of master Father was—and Father returned the compliment. My father holds a license as pilot of San Francisco harbor so he didn't even have to hire a pilot or a tugboat to get inside the Heads. The tugboat steamed alongside us at half-speed, ready to throw us a hawser if the wind died and we were forced to be towed in, but Father entered the Golden Gate, sailed past Mile Rock Light House, dipped the flag in salute to the lighthouse keeper, and came to safe anchorage off Alcatraz Island. He let go the hooks and waved a superior good-bye to the indignant tugboat captain.

There was a brisk breeze blowing over the Bay and hardly a cloud overhead. To the eastward rolled the hills of Berkeley.

"Your mother's over there, Joan. I'm going to ship you off this trip."

I stared at Father.

"You mean me leave the ship?"

He didn't look at me as he replied:

"Yes, it's high time you had a woman's care of you." That was the first he told me of his plan to send me ashore to live.

"Are you going to quit the sea too?" I was filled with terror. Not to be on the ship any more—ever? Never to steer a course under the Southern Cross—reef a sail in a storm, never to set a halyard to the rhythm of Swede's chantey?

"No. I'm goin' to stay on this ship as long as she floats. I'll stand by her until she goes down under me." He looked away from the hills out towards the sea. Little did Father realize when he spoke those words that they would come true!

I was going to live on shore with my mother and brothers and sister. I didn't even remember what my mother looked like. She was only a beautiful symbol to me—something far off and not quite real that had been painted for me in words from my father—and not some-one real that I could live with. But now I must. Father would make me. It seemed too terrible to endure.

The Quarantine officers and Customs officers passed

us. There was nothing then to keep me from going ashore. Father packed my canvas sea bag full of my belongings. It bulged with my sea boots, my oilskins and sou'wester. I wrapped my little boats carefully in burlap and carried them under my arm for they were too precious to trust to careless hands. My other treasures were a jaw of shark teeth and an octopus in a big can of alcohol.

Stitches came aft to help load my things into the dinghy to go ashore.

"Ain't you ever comin' back to us, Skipper?" Stitches asked me in a hoarse voice which was barely audible. I hadn't realized until then that I'd be leaving him behind. I couldn't leave Stitches, for I loved him.

"Can't you come to the land with me, Stitches? You can live with me for always," I said.

Stitches didn't answer me; he just sort of blew his nose and looked away.

"I'm coming back some time, Stitches," I promised. I saw his old hands shaking as he tied my bundles up. He seemed to delay the parting by fumbling around. I gave him my ships to hold and I went below to change into my dress and hair ribbon. When I came up on deck the crew had disappeared off the decks. Weren't they going to say good-bye to me? Even Stitches was nowhere to be seen.

"Come on, cast off now," Father called.

Bulgar and Oleson were in the dinghy below waiting to row Father and me ashore. I climbed up to the rail and started down the Jacob's ladder when I suddenly remembered something I had forgotten. I dashed back on deck and made for the cabin.

"Now what the hell?" called Father after me.

I grabbed my four kittens I had forgotten and put them in a flour sack, then I went up on the poop deck to where my pet seagull was in a packing-case cage.

"Come on, Old Man, we're going ashore," I told the gull as I put him under one arm. Then I swung the sack of cats over my shoulder, and once more I went to the Jacob's ladder to disembark.

What a fine bunch of barnacles the crew were, I thought, when I couldn't see them anywhere. Just as I went over the side I spotted them—Stitches was behind the mizzen mast pretending to be looking the opposite direction from me; Swede and the Jap cook were peeking out at me from the donkey-room forward. Fred Nelson acted the queerest of all of them. He appeared to be absorbed in polishing the brass on the binnacle, but he polished the one spot so steadily I thought he would wear it out.

"Hey Skipper," he called: "Here's somethin' to remember the ship by." He came down to me and handed me a plug of Star Cut Plug Tobacco. "It ain't much, but it's wishin' you a fair wind for your westin'." His face seemed white and drawn. He looked at me so hard I thought he was looking right through me.

"Pile down here and quit your dawdling," Father ordered from his seat in the dinghy.

A funny lump came in my throat. It felt as if I had swallowed too big a hunk of oatmeal and it had stuck in my windpipe. I couldn't make the feeling go away. I was afraid I would start to blubber at leaving the crew forever and especially my adored Stitches, so I yelled out very loud as I descended the Jacob's ladder:

"So long, everybody. I won't ever forget you."

14

I find navigating on shore full of shoals

IN the small boat Father asked why I had brought the gull and what was in the flour sack.

"My belongings!" I answered.

"Your mother'll never stand for that junk to clutter up her house. You're a landsman now, Joan, and things is going to be different." I couldn't understand why Father didn't give me the devil instead of talking so low and quiet-like. I thought he was glad to get rid of me because I was always such a worry to him.

The ride on the ferry boat across San Francisco Bay to get a train to Berkeley was an experience I'll never forget. A crowd gathered around me on the ferry to look at my seagull and the octopus in the can. The kittens squirmed around in their sack but I didn't open it because I was afraid they'd get away from me. I didn't realize then that I was a freak sight. I thought all the people who grouped around me wanted to be friends,

so I took them into my confidence freely. They smiled
and looked at one another as I talked. I was telling them
about the South Seas; how I got the little octopus; what
the name of our ship was. No one did any talking except me—the crowd just stared at me and listened.

At the Oakland Pier we got a train. The conductor
came along and tried to take the seagull and bag of cats
away from me. He wanted to put them in the baggage
car, but I protested, and he let me keep them. When we
arrived in Berkeley Father took a taxi from the station
up to my mother's house. I was all eyes at the surrounding view, the rolling hills, the houses with neat lawns,
trolley cars, groups of laughing boys and girls strolling
along the streets. I forgot the ship for an instant. In my
transport of joy I could think of nothing but my new life.

We got out of the cab in front of a two-story
wooden house. We walked up a path and through a gate
that had two tall posts on either side of it. On one of
them was a weather vane—a whale on a stick that spun
around in the wind. It had been there for years and
Mother used it to watch for shore winds to blow my
father home. A tangled mass of bright-colored flowers
lined the walk. A huge climbing vine with flowers the
color of South Sea coral hanging from them half covered the porch. They were roses, the first I had ever seen.
The appearance of the house made me think of a contented turtle asleep in seaweeds. I couldn't get enough of
the beauty of the garden. I felt Father's hand tugging at
my arm.

"There's your mother, Joan."

I looked up, and there I saw my mother standing in
the doorway. She was wiping her hands on her apron and

crying and laughing all at once. My first impression of her was of a round, chubby little woman—round and delicious, like a duff pudding that looked so good I could eat it. Her skin was very white, her eyes as blue as the water in a lagoon, and the wisps of grey hair that fell on her forehead reminded me of white sea spray. I couldn't take my eyes off her—my mother! I had seen her five years before when she came to a lumber camp in Oregon to see Father, but the memory of her was blurred. Father's romantic picture of her was more vivid in my mind than my actual recollection. She was so different from any woman I knew. Dressed in a faded blue house dress with a white collar fastened with a shell pink coral brooch—wiping her hands on her apron—always will that picture remain with me. I didn't know what to say to her. She was expecting her seafarers home, for Father had telephoned her from San Francisco. Was I as much of a surprise to her as she was to me? I expected my mother to be gruff like Father but her voice was gentle —she was all softness.

What did daughters do when they met their mothers?

Father threw his arms around Mother and lifted her from the floor. He hadn't seen her for five years! I felt a twinge of jealousy at being left out. I had always been most important to Father and Mother was usurping my place. She left Father's arms and gathered me to her. Her hands were so soft and smooth they felt funny as they petted me. She seemed so weak compared with sailors. Her arms didn't have as much strength as one of my toes. Physical strength was my ideal and she did not have it. I knew she was somebody wonderful but she was going to have to prove it.

"Speak to your mother," Father said.

I eyed her up and down, from truck to keel, before I answered:

"Are you going to let me have my seagull and cats here?"

Mother laughed and said:

"You can keep them in the back yard."

With that compromise settled, I let down my barriers of hostility. I don't know whether I was thrilled at being in a house that was a home or whether I was terrified. I remember I felt shut in and cramped, and my brothers and sister standing around staring at me as if I were a mirage instead of a real person didn't put me at my ease.

"Joan, you change your dress because it is dinner time. We have dinner for the boarders at twelve o'clock," was the next thing Mother said.

"I haven't got any other dress," I answered. My voice, attuned to the open sea, boomed like a cannon in that small room.

"Don't talk so loudly," cautioned Mother.

My mother, to help make both ends meet, kept boarders from the University of California.

"They are professors, dear. You can sit at the same table with them."

"Are professors all men?" I wanted to know. Mother said they were men, the ones that lived at that house.

"Because I don't like women," I added.

My sister retired from the room. She was a very proper young lady and she didn't approve of me at all. That noon I met the boarders. They were introduced to me, and then they began firing questions at me from all sides.

I thought they were nice, friendly men who were interested in the sea, until they took sides against me.

"Do you mean to tell us that YOU *saw* a native child actually being born?" came the horrified voice of the professor of economics.

"Sure I saw it. You didn't think she stopped having her baby just because I was there, did you?" I retorted. Those professors thought I was lying. What did they know about the sea, anyway? Then, contradicting another statement I had happened to make, came the retort:

"In our civilized world today there is no such thing as slave trading." The bewhiskered professor across from me brought his hand down on the table with a smack as he said it. He was trying to show me up and it got under my collar.

"The hell there ain't," I cried back at him just as hard and so much louder that he drew back in his shell.

"Sssh! Joan!" It was Mother's voice from the head of the table. I guess she thought I would drive away her boarders.

"I won't sssh!" I cried just as loud as ever. "He's trying to make me out a liar. Ask Father, he'll tell you."

"Sure there is slave trading today," said Father grudgingly. "It's called blackbirdin' in the South Seas. Some sea captains on sailin' ships take cargoes of natives and 'contract' them for a pound apiece for five years to the planters in Northern Australia. When the natives have been worked almost to death the planters pay the sea captains to take the natives back to the islands they stole them from. Instead of takin' them back to their own islands, the captains dump their loads of blacks on the first handy

island that lies in their course. That's why now you hardly
ever see a pure breed of native in any tribe—the black-
birders have mixed them up."

"Astonishing!" was the comment of the learned ques-
tioners. "Astonishing!" Mother didn't tell Father to sssh!
They didn't dare openly dispute Father so they turned
back on me. First they asked about storms at sea, adventures on our voyages—then they disbelieved them. The
professor of economics was the worst.

"You are a very interesting study, little girl." He rose
from the table leaving me feeling like a germ under a
microscope. I could see that navigating wasn't going to be
so easy with those landlubbers.

That night I slept for the first time in my life in a
regular bed. The sheets felt so tickly and cool and the
mattress was soft, but I couldn't sleep. The house was so
still and it didn't rock! The stillness made me feel seasick.
I couldn't hear the noise of feet on deck above me. My
bird and cats were in the hold, or rather what is called
on shore, the cellar of the house. And so I lay awake
most of the night pitching and tossing and wishing the
house would just rock a little bit so I could go to sleep.

The following morning I was up at daybreak. I dressed
quickly and ran through the house calling:

"All hands on deck. It's four bells!"

Father came out of his room and caught me by the
back of the neck.

"Pipe down, you. There's folks asleep," he said. It was
time to eat breakfast according to ship schedule. The
boarders were awakened by my cries. Mother served
them their breakfast as soon as she could prepare it.
When she called breakfast I dashed to the table and

grabbed the biggest portion of scrambled eggs and a stack
of pancakes and began scoffing them.

"Where are your manners?" It was Mother speaking
as she took my self-helping away from me.

"I got here first," I protested, "and it's first come first
get!" But Mother just couldn't understand.

There followed a series of days full of bewildering
problems for me. The other children on our block, instead of playing with me as I used to dream children
would, drew away from me.

"She swears bad words," I heard one girl tell another.

"That girl off the ship is too rough, my mother says,"
confided her little friend. And so it went. Why didn't
they like me? Here were children my own age and I
didn't know how to play with them. Everything I said or
did sent them away from me. My own sister and my
brothers found excuses to take them away to their friends,
leaving me behind. Running her boarding house kept
Mother constantly busy and Father was at the ship all
day long. When he came home in the evenings it was
Mother he naturally turned to. I seemed forgotten. Oh,
how I longed for a storm to arise to blow away the fear
and loneliness of the land. I couldn't stay in the house
because it crushed me down and the professors didn't
approve of me. I kept out in the backyard as much as I
could. Everything was so different on land. My seagull
died the second day I was home. I tried to replace it with
love for the chickens Mother kept. But chickens couldn't
fly. They seemed as bound down to the earth as I was,
away from the ship. Even the roses in the garden had
thorns on them. The lilies in the islands were soft-
stemmed and lovely. I couldn't bear it. I wouldn't obey

my mother because I knew she wasn't strong enough to
lick me. Every night Father came home from the ship
and she would tell him how difficult I was to handle.

"She is your child. You'll have to handle her," I heard
her tell Father.

"Joan will get used to land ways soon, Mother, don't
you worry about her."

I heard Father and Mother discussing me.

"You raised her—so perhaps you can discipline her,"
Mother said.

"Joan is your daughter. If you try to understand her
she'll steer as easy as a full-rigger in a fair wind," came
back Father.

"She'll drive all my boarders away. Last night I heard
her ask one of the professors if he had ever gone through
a shark's guts with his hands." Mother was horrified as
she related the facts to Father. Instead of finding sym-
pathetic ears for the story of my disgraceful conduct,
Mother saw Father laughing.

"As if that wasn't bad enough Joan said this was a hell
of a house because there wasn't a bedbug or a cockroach
in it. I tell you, you'll have to speak to her."

I couldn't understand why Mother thought that I was
terrible because I acted as I did. She went on:

"The child insists on practising spitting through a
crack in the back fence at the woman next door."

Poor Mother! At that time I wondered why she was
so distressed. Now that the first glamour was gone, I
looked upon my sister and brothers as jelly fish because
they couldn't lick me or climb or spit or swear for beans.
I had been home, "on land" as I termed it, for three
weeks when Father announced that he was going to sail.

Mother packed his sea bag. Father never had a suitcase. He always used his own sea "ditty bags."

A shot of agony went through me when I realized he was leaving, and without me. I couldn't bear it. I wouldn't stay on the land. Unable to contain myself I ran to my father and kicked him in the pants to make him notice me more than he noticed Mother.

"Say, ain't I going with you?" I pleaded.

Father looked at me in a puzzled way, as if he didn't know how to answer me, then he said:

"I'm just getting ready to sail, Joan. Thought I'd get my things on board all ready in case we get a fair wind that'll take us out without any towboat."

That settled it for me. I'd run away. If he thought he could leave me on land while he sailed off to the South Seas again he'd be mistaken. My sense of navigation came in handy. I remembered how we came from San Francisco to Berkeley. I'd go back to San Francisco the same way, but I didn't have any money. That night when the house was asleep I sneaked into my father's room and got his pants. I stole a big silver dollar from them and kept it in my fist all night. It was my price to freedom. The following morning while Mother was busy, and after my brothers and sister had started for work or school, I left home. Without hat or coat I took shore leave from the house with only my four kittens for company and went to San Francisco. I found my way to the dock opposite our schooner which lay at anchorage and I told a fisherman that I belonged on the *Minnie A. Caine.*

"Will you row me out for this much money?" I asked, and I showed him a half dollar in change. The old fisherman grinned and told me to get in his row boat, and he pulled me out to the ship, but he wouldn't take my money. I climbed on deck and bumped smack into Stitches. The old man's eyes nearly popped out in joy at seeing me again.

"I knowed the Old Man wouldn't let you stay ashore. I know he'd bring you back," he repeated over and over like a chant.

"He didn't bring me back. I ran away." I didn't even ask Stitches not to tell. He hid me in the lazarette in a bed of old canvas. The Jap cook brought me some bread and a big can of soup. Fred Nelson was the only one of the crew who didn't volunteer to help deceive my father about me. He came down to speak to me, but I guess he forgot what he wanted to say because his only words were:

"It ain't much company for you, kid, these rats what live down here," and so saying he turned on his heel and went back on deck. I stayed down in the dark hold all day, but I would have stayed there forever rather than go back to the land where everything I did was wrong. Along about six o'clock I heard Father's voice on the poop deck above me.

"I'll break every goddamned one of your necks if you don't tell me where she is," he said.

I heard Swede and Stitches and the Jap cook stalling.

"I know she came back here. She wouldn't go no place else, so out with it. Where is she hiding?" he demamded. I heard each of the crew deny over and over that they knew anything about me, then I heard a scuffle. Father was beating some one of them up. I might just as well give up, I concluded, so I climbed out of the lazarette on deck. I faced an angry father.

"What the hell's the idea?" he shouted at me, but somehow I didn't feel he was as mad as he looked.

"If I let you give me a good licking, can I stay?" I asked. I would rather have died on that ship than give up. The crew gave me a look with one accord that seemed to say: "You've made liars of us." But strangely enough, Father didn't try to punish them.

"Get forrard about your duties. What are you loafin' around here for?" he roared at them. Father gave me a licking with a rope's end and I swear it felt good. It was like old times again, but when he had finished he took me ashore. My mother was very silent that night. I ate my supper in the kitchen and went to bed without speaking to her.

I was up at daylight the next morning, but I wasn't soon enough for Father. He had left for the ship an hour before. I went outside and a strong wind was blowing. The sky was clear and I could see the blue water of the bay from our front porch. In the backyard was a giant eucalyptus tree. I climbed it with as much ease as I could scale the rigging on the ship. The higher I climbed the farther I could see out the Golden Gate. From my perch on the peak of the tree, I saw the ships at anchor in the bay. One of them was my ship. That wind meant Father would set sail. He was going without me! I found myself crying inside-like and I kept saying:

"Don't leave me on land, Father! Come back and get me! Please, oh, please don't let me die of loneliness here on land."

I didn't take my eyes off the distant harbor. I stared through the cold wind until my eyes burned with pain. I must have been up there for about three hours. I was hoping against hope that Father would hear me calling to him to come back and get me, when through my daze I heard my mother's voice far below me at the root of the tree calling to me to come down. But I wouldn't come down. Maybe our ship would sail if I took my eyes off the bay. Maybe I wouldn't see her go. After a while Mother quit calling and went away.

A loud clanging of bells broke into my spell. Glancing below I saw a big red firewagon in front of the house. Firemen were rigging up two ladders against the tree and three of the men climbed up after me. Mother had called out the fire department, to get me down.

"I won't come down," I warned. "Go away and leave me alone."

Instead of coming down I climbed one branch higher. I would stay there until I dropped. The wind was like a soothing hand to my bewildered mind. Up there it was friendly. Silly little fool that I was, I thought the land was all off its keel and it was really only me. I couldn't adjust myself to foreign surroundings.

But soon, how soon I don't remember, I heard my father's voice bellowing up at me:

"On deck, you!" That was all he called, but I came down the tree like a sailor shaken off the foot ropes in a storm.

"Yes, sir?" I said when I faced him on the ground, surrounded by a frantic group of neighbors who had been attracted by the firewagon. There was great confusion and explanations. I stuck to my story that I thought he was sailing without me. My mother didn't say anything. She looked as if she was crying inside.

"Take Joan back to the sea. She'll fret herself away

here," she told Father when we went in the house.

"What makes you think I want her?" Father came back.

"You've been delaying sailing for a week. Your cargo is on board; you've had fair winds off shore; now you come and tell me your sailors have refused to ship out with you because Joan's leaving is a bad omen—and yet you didn't fight about it. If you told the truth to yourself it would be that you don't want to go without Joan. Take her back with you."

I could have kissed my mother, and I would have if I hadn't thought it was too sissy to do it.

Father hotly denied that he had held up sailing on account of me, but he didn't look mother in the eye when he blustered:

"I'm sailin' on the flood tide tonight, Mother, and Joan goes with me."

True to his word Father sailed that night and I was on board. After helping set sail, I climbed to the crosstrees where I watched the receding lights of the harbor disappear into a foggy bank of night. A snorting breeze carried us out the Golden Gate past the Farallone Islands, and beyond the moan of the bell buoy on the shoals. Our bow was pointed due west. The jib-boom plunged under rising swells and shook itself free. The ship rolled and groaned as if she were relieved in her freedom from anchorage. I heard six bells ring below, and the watch was set. Nelson was at the wheel, Stitches was singing on the fo'c's'le head, and the dim glow of Father's pipe traced his paces from the binnacle to the rail and back, and I, up in the spanker crosstrees thumbed my nose at the land we left far astern.

15

From the region of floating mountains of ice to the Island of White
Natives

"WE'LL have to dodge the hurricanes south of the
Equator this trip," said my father to the mate, as we
sailed out of Adelaide, South Australia, with a load of
salt for the States. "With a dead weight on board of wet
salt it'll be too dangerous to try to outride the storms at
this time of the year."

It was April—just the beginning of tropic winter time.
By the time we had sailed south of Tasmania and had
circled the South Island of New Zealand, which would
take about two months, we would be right in the midst of
the worst weather of the year.

"We better get the fog horn out and the riding lights
trimmed if you're going to take that south passage, Captain," observed the mate. "Them fogs and mists from the
Antarctic are mean beggars."

I was soon to find out why the mate referred to the Antarctic as mean. Father had set a course around to the southward of Tasmania. For three weeks we sailed with fair wind and clear skies, and then the fair wind gradually changed to a stinging sharpness. The skies misted up in a sort of transparent fog, and mirages appeared on the horizon. Mirrored against the indefinite horizon were two islands with tropical foliage seemingly floating in space. The mirage is a dangerous thing to mariners, for it confuses even the most careful navigation.

"Joan, you ain't much use, you go on the fo'c's'le head and turn the foghorn, three short blasts a minute, then one long one," said my father.

"Are you afraid of running into another vessel down here?" I asked.

"Not a chance of sighting even a hunk of driftwood, but the marine law says we have to squawk a foghorn when we get in the iceberg region."

I had never seen an iceberg, and I was over-eager to be on the lookout on the fo'c's'le head to sight the first one. Our foghorn was a contraption that looked like a big coffee grinder. It was green with tarnish and thick with rust. I took my position just port of the capstan and ground away. I was rewarded by a rasping grunt. It took all my strength to spin the handle around just to make one blast. In spite of the cold I soon got very warm trying to make the three short and one long blasts come. Father came forward and watched me straining away on it. He grinned at my exhaustion and said he thought that would keep me out of deviltry for a while, or make me so tired that I'd be willing to sleep and give him a respite from watching me.

The noise of the horn began to echo back at me in an eerie tone. I called to Father:

"We must be near land. The echo is coming back at me strong."

He dashed to the fo'c's'le head, and peered into the thickening mush of fog. The sea was so still that every sound became magnified. In a few minutes the suck-suck sound of water washing against some bulk came to our ears.

"Drop the topsails," he bellowed, "bring her around." With a violent jerk, the ship came up in the wind and stopped. Ahead of us, not more than five hundred yards away, loomed a giant iceberg. As we watched it, it sank deep in the black water and then, as if it were some living beast, it heaved high out of the sea. The swish of the water around it, the suction of its movements, made a dangerous current. We began to drift nearer to it. Our ship had no power except that of the sails, and the wind had dropped and left them limp and powerless.

"Throw over the kedge anchors," Father ordered. Kedge anchors are small, and used for emergency cases. The men rushed aft and threw one over each side the vessel. They gave weight and pulled us back from drifting head on to the iceberg. For a few minutes they held, but the water around us was a seething mass of cross currents. Other bergs, larger and deeper, were in the offing. We had run into a whole nest of them. A steamer could have backed away, turned around, and left the place of danger, but our ship was helpless to move. The bergs made deep valleys, and whatever wind there was was cut off by their height. The water sounded as if it were boiling around us. The mate threw over a chip of wood

to see which way we were drifting, but the chip just
whirled around and went down. A typhoon would have
been a welcome visitor then, for at least its wind would
have carried us away—but just being becalmed, waiting
for the jaws of the iceberg to finish us, was like a terrible
nightmare.

The cabin-boy and the Jap cook crouched behind the
galley, pale and shaking with fright. Father's face was
set grimly. A frozen death awaited us. Things at sea
seem to take on human qualities. The perversity of the
wind was the curse of some dead sea captain, and
baffling calms were from the souls of lost sailors. That
nearest iceberg was like a sea beast gloating over us as its
prey.

"All hands on deck!" went the cry from Father, and
it was repeated down the fo'c's'le. The men came scram-
bling up, buttoning their oilskins and sou'westers around
themselves closely. When they were all ready Father
turned to them:

"You've got one chance in a thousand to get out of here
with your lives. Throw overboard the cargo."

In a flash the crew were tearing away the battens off
the hatches. If the heavy cargo was thrown overboard,
the ship would ride lighter and higher on the waves, and
the impact from a smash would be lessened. The curses
of the men in the hold as they chucked up sacks of salt
beat a staccato on the still air.

"Joan, you and the cook and cabin-boy load up the
lifeboat. Put tins of hardtack, a keg of water and a tar-
paulin in it." With those instructions he took his post at
the fo'c's'le head and watched our ship go nearer the
bergs. Two frigate birds with long spiked tails hovered

above. A frantic little mother-carries-her-chicken bird flew around and around in a dizzy circle near the stern. And Father just waited! With each roll of the ship we came nearer. The crew worked throwing out the sacks of salt like men possessed, and the ship lightened.

Father ordered the rope bumpers put out, and two cork buoys lowered over the bowsprit to break the crash if we hit the iceberg. The ship wouldn't answer to the rudder, for the currents were more powerful. Just as we braced ourselves for the destroying collision we were caught in an eddy that lifted us high on the water and sent our ship dizzily about one hundred yards past the iceberg. Our relief was so great that we didn't mind the loss of cargo.

All night long we drifted in the ice floes, miraculously avoiding being crushed by them.

The following morning we found ourselves afloat in a world of white icebergs and thick mist. It seemed as though we were at the end of the world. It was difficult for Father to figure out our position, as there was no sun, and to navigate by dead reckoning was useless as the log line couldn't register how much we had drifted in the cross currents. For a week that continued—breathless days and nights that were ghostly in those white canyons of frozen water.

Sometimes in the night we could hear the screech of sea birds leaving the ice, and then silence again.

Whenever any real danger was upon us my father used to whistle or sing, or play his old water-soaked violin. I asked him how he could be so gay when death was staring us all in the face, and he said:

"What the hell do you expect me to do, bawl about

it? Besides, if the crew hear me singin' they'll think there's nothin' to be afraid of and it keeps their guts from freezin' inside of them."

He sang often in the two weeks that followed as we blindly picked our way out of the iceberg region. The first time the sun shone after that was about three hundred miles southeast of New Zealand. A stiff breeze cleared the sky, and our sails bellied out tautly under it.

"We'll sail due East, Mr. Swanson," Father said to the mate, "and try and make Pitcairn. I haven't been there for years and I want Joan to see it."

I had heard the name of Pitcairn Island all my life. Every sailor looks upon it as the haven for seafarers. From their descriptions it was the one perfect spot on earth, free from worries, money, and work.

Old Stitches used to tell me about Pitcairn and its qualities of a paradise, but I thought it was the ravings of a mind that had had too much liquor and too many girls in port.

"What are we going to see on Pitcairn?" I asked my father.

"White natives. It's the only South Sea island that has a tribe of English-speaking, light-skinned inhabitants."

I was thrilled at the prospect of visiting Pitcairn— for white people were more of a curiosity to me than natives. As our ship nosed her way across the sea towards Pitcairn, I spent many hours listening to tales about that strange island from my father and two old sailors who had been there often.

When Kipling gave to the world his much overquoted lines, "East is East and West is West and never the twain shall meet," he probably forgot that in the most remote part of the South Seas, East and West had met and had formed a race of people, living in a high degree of civilization and in a community almost free from sin—to disprove his theory.

I looked up the island on the chart, and found it marked there with an inconsequential dot, and flaunting the austere name of "Pitcairn, 23 degrees S. latitude, 120 W. longitude." By latitude and longitude I can locate a spot on the ocean as accurately as a landlubber can find 42nd Street and Broadway.

Father saw me studying the chart, and observed:

"On the approach from the southeast the island looks like a cone of rock juttin' out of the sea. Some times mariners call it 'Neptune's Thimble' because of its resemblance to a thimble in shape."

"How did anybody get on a rock island so far away from the big island groups?" I asked.

"I'll tell you, Joan, because I think you ought to know the whole romance of Pitcairn. Lots of folks has written about it, but none of them know all the facts like we sailormen know."

"Have the islanders been there forever?" I wanted to know.

"Nope. You see in the year 1789 His Majesty's Ship *Bounty* was sent out from England to the South Seas to gather breadfruit trees for the purpose of transplantin' the same in the British West Indies. In command of the *Bounty* was a tyrannical, overbearin' taskmaster, a regular s.o.b. His name was Lieutenant William Bligh, and the crew was afraid of him, and at the same time they hated his guts.

"For months there had been a seething undercurrent of revolt brewing in the fo'c's'le, and it was led by the ship's carpenter, a Mr. Christian. They laid their plans carefully for mutiny—but they bided their time until the *Bounty* sailed into the vicinity of Tahiti."

"What good would it do to mutiny in the South Seas?" I asked, for I knew that escape in the islands was almost impossible for a white man fugitive on English possessions.

"Huh," snorted Father, "those bastards were so sore on Old Man Bligh they didn't give a damn what became of them just so as they got rid of him and his officers." And from Father I learned how the "white native island" was founded.

When Mr. Christian learned from one of the officers that the *Bounty* was about two hundred miles off Tahiti he gave the signal for the mutiny. With more daring than the pirates of the Arabian Nights the crew mutinied. They bound and gagged the captain and those officers that were loyal to him, and set them adrift in the open sea in the ship's cutter which they had provisioned and watered. Christian assumed command of the *Bounty* and her mutineers.

The abandoned captain and officers drifted for weeks through uncharted, shark-infested waters. They circumvented a dangerous coral shoal to land on what appeared to be a fertile uncharted island, only to be driven from there by the cannibalistic inhabitants. After a time their supplies ran short, and they subsisted on turtle, sun-dried fish—and saved the raindrops for water.

Bligh was stricken with a peculiar malady from the strain and exposure. His officers had to save his life be-

cause he alone knew how to navigate, and that little
cutter had to make some port soon, or their goose was
cooked. They didn't dare land on any of the islands that
weren't charted because they might run into a nest of
cannibals again.

Nowadays we have charts and surveys of the islands,
but in 1789 a lot of these atolls were never heard of.

They had to get some fresh water and food for Bligh
or he'd die on them, so one night the officers put into an
atoll island and stole fresh fruits and coconuts to nourish him. Weeks drifted into months and at the end of five
months they reached New Guinea, a distance of three
thousand five hundred miles from where they were set
adrift. From New Guinea they secured passage on a trading schooner to Australia. Lieutenant Bligh lost no time
in informing His Majesty of their predicament. Some
time later he was rewarded by being appointed Governor
of New South Wales.

Indignant upon learning of the mutiny of his sailors,
King George ordered H.M.S. *Pandora* sent to the scene
of the rebellion.

In the meantime the *Bounty* was cruising around the
South Seas looking for a place to land and at the same
time avoid capture. Fourteen of the *Bounty* crew who
had mutinied went ashore at Tahiti and took up native
lives in preference to being "stretched by the neck" by His
Majesty's officers if they were caught. Besides, those
fourteen men preferred a life among beautiful native
girls to that of hard work on shipboard. They used poor
judgment, however, for the officers of the *Pandora* found
them and took them prisoners. They were chained like
dogs to the stanchions of the ship, and put on rations of

bread and water. The *Pandora* set sail for England where a death penalty would have been dealt to the mutineers, but she struck a submerged coral reef and became a total wreck. That reef is now known as Pandora Reef on the charts. While the *Pandora* was smashing to pieces on the sharp reef, the officers tried to get away, but they made no attempt to free the prisoners from their chains and they left them to a miserable slow death. They didn't give them the fighting chance that the mutineers had given Bligh and his men.

Christian had sailed the *Bounty* to Ruratu. His men grew so restless and lonely, that he advised them each to take to himself a native wife. Fascinated by the white skin of the sailors, their peculiar clothing and strange language, the young native girls looked upon them as gods, and showered gifts of fruit and flowers upon them. Mr. Christian, acting in the capacity of minister, conducted the ceremony, and each man became a husband to a native girl.

The Chief of Ruratu had a daughter Loa-Lea of unusual beauty who offered herself to Christian. This so angered the old Chief that he was planning to exterminate every white man of the crew, along with their native wives who had set a bad example for his Loa-Lea. His plans were frustrated in their inception because Loa-Lea loved the Lily-Man, or "he of the white skin" as she termed Christian, because he treated her with such kindness—such respect. To be treated with deference was a new experience to her, for native women have little or no importance in a tribe other than as creatures of convenience and producers of sons.

Loa-Lea brought news of her father's plan to exter-

minate them to her "lily-man," and Christian secretly
departed in the night with all his men, their native wives
and Loa-Lea, whom he married.

Christian had heard that the seas were being combed
for them, and so he sailed far to the westward to escape
His Majesty's forces. Just as our ship was heading now,
the *Bounty* was heading. Fifteen hundred miles south of
the Equator and about the same distance west of the coast
of South America, they came upon an uninhabited island.

They had great difficulty in finding a way to land on
the island, as there was no beach and the cliffs were almost perpendicular. Christian and a handful of men went
ashore to explore the island's possibilities. On the east
end they found a cove, overlooked by a plateau, which
had the semblance of great steps up the side of the cliff,
as if some sea giant had carved them for doorsteps to
his castle. On the table top of the island they found an
abundance of fresh fruits, water in springs, and wild
birds.

Christian returned to the *Bounty,* called his people together and impressed upon them that if they landed on
that island it was to be forever, as he intended to destroy
the *Bounty,* and with it gone there would be no means of
escape. With one accord the mutineers agreed to col-
onize the island of rock. They named it after General
Pitcairn.

The mutineers set about to strip the *Bounty* of all metal
which they would use ashore. They set their supplies
adrift on rafts to float in shore. Those who did not swim
in went to the landing in small boats. When the last man
had left the vessel, Christian lashed the helm amidships,
headed her bow directly into the island and deserted her.

Gathered on the cliff of their new colony, the crew watched the ground swells of the Pacific wash the *Bounty* in toward the cliffs, until with a mighty crash she struck the wall and sank into the unsounded depth of the sea. Gone forever was their hope of ever leaving the island, but also, gone forever was any evidence of the *Bounty* to betray them into the hands of His Majesty's officers.

Each man and wife set about and built a hut and portioned off a plot of land for a home. Every variety of tropical fruit and berries grew in great profusion. There was more than enough of everything for everybody. But in spite of that all did not run smoothly on Pitcairn. Christian was chief. The Bible was the only form of government. Their religion was and is to this day Seventh Day Adventism.

In time children were born to the mutineers by the native wives, and the children were white. South Sea natives have intermarried so much for generations that their blood is depleted and the white man's blood predominated.

The sailors call Pitcairn Eden, and rightly perhaps, because a woman was the cause of a quarrel which proved fatal to the whites. One of the mutineers, a Mr. McCoy, had sent his wife to gather sea bird eggs from the rocks on the edge of the cliff. Losing her foothold she fell a thousand feet to the reef below and was instantly killed. As there was only an equal number of women and men, and all of them married, the mutineer, when he became lonely, took to himself the wife of one of the men. That so angered the husband that he killed his wife. McCoy became an outcast, and all the husbands looked upon him as a danger to their happiness. From that time

on dissension and intrigue flourished. Several of the mutineers set out in a small boat to find another island, and
that left McCoy, Christian, a Charles Adams, and seven
other whites with their native wives on the island. The
natives there now are the descendants of those families.

Those whites and natives have a colony now without
quarrels. They are industrious and God-fearing—but
lockjaw is rapidly wiping them out.

. . . .

The mate came up on the poop deck to where Father
was sitting and asked,

"Shall we give the Pitcairn Islanders some rope and
canvas this trip, Captain?"

We were only about fifty miles from Pitcairn, and by
nine o'clock that evening we would be hove to off it.

"Yes. We've lost our cargo, so we might as well divide
up our supplies."

The Pitcairn Islanders wait months and months for
sailing ships to come. Very few ships ever go so far off
the beaten sailing tracks, and when one does, the islanders offer up devout thanksgiving. Along about nine
o'clock, Pitcairn loomed ahead. On the top of it fires
were burning. First they appeared on one end of the
island, then on the other. They had sighted us. The fires
were beacon lights to us, so that we would not strike the
shoals by sailing in too close.

"Give them the freedom of the ship when they come
aboard," Father instructed the mate. "These natives
never steal anythin'."

Within an hour from the time we hove to, three boats
from Pitcairn were alongside, and about thirty-five islanders came on board. I studied them closely for signs

of native blood, but they were as white as I am. They spoke English, simply, and with a peculiar accent. The women were delighted to see me, another white woman. One old dame stroked my hair; a young girl offered to trade her native fibre dress for a pair of overalls.

We went up behind the companionway and swapped the clothes. She thought she had made a grand bargain as she strutted around with my faded blue overalls on. She ran down on the main deck and brought back a tall, quiet young woman, who seemed to be revered by the natives.

"This is Frances McCoy, who is saving our people." Miss McCoy placed both hands on my shoulders— a custom of greeting probably inherited from her native maternal ancestors.

"Did you have a peaceful voyage?" she asked, and her voice was smooth and quiet.

"No. We had the goddamndest trip we've ever had. We struck icebergs south of Tasmania and had to shoot our cargo of salt to hell."

Miss McCoy turned away from me quickly and looked off to sea, but didn't speak. McLean, who had heard me talking came over to me and said:

"They never swear on Pitcairn, Skipper," he explained. I had offended her. On Pitcairn gentleness rules, and cursing is against their law. I couldn't see how people could express themselves without cussing—but anyhow I watched myself with a terrific strain in my following conversations.

The young native girl in my overalls asked me:

"Have you any books to give to us?"

I was surprised that "white natives" could read, but I

was anxious to make amends for my swearing, and asked
her and Miss McCoy to come down in the cabin and help
themselves. The only books we had on board at that time
were books on navigation, a doctor book, and a partial
set of the Encyclopedia Britannica with those volumes
from N to S missing.

"You can take all of these," I told them, "and the books
on navigation and the charts if you want them." Miss
McCoy grabbed for the doctor book.

"My people are being wiped out by lockjaw," she
said, "and I am studying medicine from books that passing ships give me, so that I can cure them."

That was why she was so revered by the natives. She
was to save their lives!

"For years our people have begged nails and canvas
and ropes from ships so that we can get enough material
to make a ship to sail away in to the mainland. I am going in to get medicine and I will bring it back here to
stop the deaths caused by lockjaw. There is a kind of a
thorn, which when it pricks a person, gives him lockjaw," she explained. No wonder Frances McCoy, the
descendant of a pirate and mutineer, is looked upon as a
saint there.

Out of gratitude for the books and charts I gave them,
the two women gave me a beautiful screen made of skele-
ton leaves, painted with the juice of wild berries and a
small chest of carved coral. After our bargain was made,
we joined the others on the hatches on the main deck. One
of the descendants of Christian was asking about the war.

"In the Bible we read of far-off countries going to
war against each other. Is England at war now? A sailing
captain of a German full-rigged ship stopped off here

about three months ago and said he would never again trade with us."

I hadn't heard anything about the war that I could understand. I knew that the price of copra had gone up because "soldier's foods were preserved with copra oil," but it was just as indefinite in my mind what war was as it was in the minds of the natives.

Then the conversation skipped from war to music. One of the men asked if we had an organ to give them.

"What in the hell is the use of an organ in the South Sea Islands?" I asked. The "hell" had slipped out, but young Christian answered before anyone noticed it:

"We had one but the salt air has rusted it, so now it will give no music. Next time you come here will you bring to us another organ?"

I guess the Pitcairn Islanders thought in America we could pick organs off trees or something, so naïve and sincere were their requests.

At about midnight Father told the natives they would have to leave. Sadly they departed, begging us to sail to them again, and thanking us for our gifts to them. A Pitcairn Islander, when he is making a trade, doesn't drive a bargain like regular natives. They put down a commodity such as two bunches of bananas in front of you, and then they say:

"I have made you a present. Now please, you will make me a present."

It is our cue to give them a "present" in return, and if it doesn't meet with their approval, they take back their present and say, "I do not make you a present."

I was triumphant as we sailed away from the island

of white natives. I had a dress instead of overalls, feather fans, the screen and a box of coral.

Father was leaning against the spanker mast watching the sails belly out in the wind when I went to him.

"Hey, look, Father, all I got just for a few old charts and books," and I displayed my treasures.

"Charts? What the hell are you talking about?" he shouted.

"I gave them all the old charts I could find below and the books on navigation and they gave me all these things," I explained.

He didn't stop to hear any more. He took me by the back of the neck and almost carried me down in the cabin.

"Now what did you give them?"

I pointed to the empty place where the charts had been.

"How in the hell can I navigate now?" he shouted. This sounds calm as I write it, but Father wasn't calm. His face was blue he was so mad.

"I've heard you tell the sailors lots of times you were so good at navigating that you didn't need charts," I answered.

I was sorry a moment later I had traded away my overalls for that native dress, as the dress was no protection for the rope's end that tattooed my behind. I got a licking, but Father to this day has never bragged about his navigating abilities where I could hear him! But he was too stubborn to go back to the island for his charts. He had to steer by dead reckoning the rest of the trip.

After that visit to Pitcairn, I could see why everyone who has been there wants to go back. Maybe I'll go there again some day myself. I have heard since that Frances

McCoy finally got off the island in a boat which took the natives three years to build, to America. She landed in Seattle, where she began to study medicine as she had dreamed. However, within three months of the time she landed in Seattle she died a pitiful death of brain fever. She was not accustomed to the noise and confusion and strange life of cities and it struck her down before she could attain her ambition of mercy.

16

The clouds came down and the sea reached up to meet them and out of their travail a sea monster was born!

I HAD settled down for a snooze on the mizzen hatch, bored by the monotony of a dull tropic afternoon, when Father's voice shook the air with a "Clew up the topsails! Down with the foremain and mizzen!"

"Aye aye!" came from the mate on watch. "Aye aye!" echoed the sailors forward, as they ran to their places at the several ropes. We were taken "aback." Slap! smack! went the sails against the rigging as the wind caught them from the opposite tack.

"Sheet in the jibs!" Father took the wheel from the helmsman and sent him forward to lend a hand on the halyards. I leaped up the ladder to the poop deck. The wind had begun to hum with a vicious steadiness from leeward. The sky darkened over with rioting grey clouds and the sea became a funereal black.

Over the roar of the wind and the falling sails, Father alled·

"Waterspout to leeward!"

I looked where he pointed and saw the horizon in turmoil. As I watched, the clouds appeared to come down and the sea reach up to meet them. It was as though the great God of Storms had mated the sky and the sea in anger so that out of the resulting travail might be born the "terror of the sea."—Then, swaying and bending like a thing alive, whirling always with tremendous momentum, a gigantic hourglass sped with terrific pace across the waters, wearing blackness about it like a woman's trailing cloak. To me its base seemed the horizon, its top the middle of the sky and its path led straight across our bow.

"Get the wind under your tail and give a hand here," called Father.

"What's going to happen?" I yelled.

"We'll all be sucked to hell if we cross its course. This damned wind is shooting us right into the belly of the spout."

I grabbed half of the spanker boom tackle and tried to sheet in its slack. As the sail luffed I got in a few feet, only to lose them when the ship rolled back to leeward and snatched the ropes from my hands.

"Pull in the tackle," ordered Father as if he were commanding a regular sailor. I gritted my teeth and hauled again, but in vain. The wind was too strong for my single strength. Closer swept the waterspout, swelling and reaching like a living monster eager to destroy relentlessly anything in its path.

Down on the deck the men sweated and heaved on the ropes to get down the sails. Still the ship went forward, the current and wind taking us ahead at the rate of two

knots an hour with no sails up, except the truant spanker
sail that I couldn't haul in. I heard Swede groaning and
calling a breathless chantey as he led his watch lashing
down the main boom. Bulgar, Nelson and McLean were
straddled on the foot ropes of the jibboom struggling to
lash down the jibs which flapped and ballooned.

It was all chance and our fate rested in the lap of the
gods.

Now there are all sorts of sea traditions and superstitions about waterspouts. Some grave scientists who never
went to sea write learnedly that a waterspout does not and
cannot sink a ship. But no sailor ever would agree with
those scientists and when you consider on the one hand
that waterspouts are tornadoes on the ocean and on the
other hand see what tornadoes do to cities on the land the
justice of the sailor's attitude seems evident. A spout starts
when a whirling, funnel-shaped cloud hanging from a
bunch of storm clouds dips down and hits the water. The
swirling wind starts a swirl of water and just as the land
tornado picks up a house and drops it a quarter of a mile
away, so the water tornado picks up its swirling column
of water and carries it along. Surface fish, driftwood,
anything in its path goes up to tear, like a huge hourglass,
across the sea. But so temperamental is the sea tornado
that anything which changes the current of air, will
break its hold and the swirling upraised column collapses,
dropping its tons on tons of water back into the sea to
crush anything beneath.

And, caught apparently right in the path of our waterspout, that was the fate we faced. It is funny in a crisis
how little things catch your attention. With that waterspout racing toward us on the wind, the men had to cling

on with their knees and stomachs to keep from being whisked off into the sea. I had never seen any of our crew show such real fear in my life. They were as pale as the white canvas they were trying to reef in, for a waterspout was no ordinary hazard. No calculations or navigations could estimate what dizzy course it might take. I found myself listening to the frenzied cries of the sea birds that came down from the sky to seek the protection of the sea against the angry chaos of the air above. Whenever sea birds fly low on the water in a storm it is proof that the winds of the heavens are too vicious—too conflicting for their wings. Rats leaving a sinking ship are not as fatal a sign to mariners as defeated sea birds. The smaller birds lasted longer under the beating of the wind than the big ones. An albatross, with a spread of six feet of wings, flapped helplessly in the valley of the swells.

For the first time in the midst of danger my father didn't sing. He bit his lips together in grim determination and never once took his eye off the fast approaching waterspout. He turned the helm and threw the ship into the belly of the swells, a move that no sane navigator would do under ordinary conditions, for a vessel is at the mercy of the sea once she loses her balance in the trough of the breakers.

With almost an agonized screech he called the crew aft:

"For the love of Christ get this spanker in before we go nose in to croaking." Swede, the mate, Oleson and Mc-Lean, who had come in off the jibboom, clambered up the deck. They hauled on the spanker tackle. The rope wouldn't give to their pulls. A knot had become tangled in the block on the end of the boom, and that boom was swinging out over the sea about fifteen feet.

"Send a man out to clear it," ordered Father. Nelson volunteered.

"Now hold on out there," the mate advised him as he started out the swinging tackle, holding on with his feet and shinnying along like a monkey on a stick. Once when the vessel rolled heavily the boom dipped to the water and the waves lapped Nelson, almost sucking him under. But he held fast. The other sailors stood at position on deck ready to haul it in the second the block was free.

After what seemed hours, but in fact was only a few moments, Nelson called: "Take it away," and with one accord the men on deck began to pull in the truant boom. Nelson hung on to the boom as they pulled it in. The boom on a big ship is handled very much as you handle the boom on a little fishing boat. There is a pulley block fastened to the end of the boom and a pulley block fastened to the deck and the boom is controlled by three strands of tackle running over the two blocks, the free end of the tackles being cleated down on the deck. To help in the handling of the boom as it swings over and to ease the strain, the block on deck is fastened to a steel coupling which slides along a three foot steel rod riveted at each end to the deck. This coupling is enclosed in a steel lined wooden box or hood to protect the coupling from rusting. The block itself is outside the hood and slides along the top of the grooved opening. The wind had eased a little and the boom began to swing over so fast that the tackle showed a few feet of slack. However, the strain had been so heavy that the steel coupling had jammed slightly at the end of the rail. McLean reached down in the opening at the top of the hood to push the

steel coupling free and hurry the boom over. Then the
wind suddenly veered back a point, caught the spanker
and slung it over the side again with a terrific jolt. A
gruesome shriek of pain split the roar of the wind and
rattle of ropes and McLean fell in a heap over the hood.
His arm, just above the elbow, had been caught and
crushed in the grip of the steel coupling. The wind backed
up the force of the boom that held taut the tackles.

McLean was moaning. I heard a stifled, agonised "O
Jesus" come from him. But a man's life is of little consequence when the fate of a ship is at stake. That boom
had to be hauled in or lost, no matter what happened to
McLean. But with the man's arm crushed in the jammed
coupling and his body lying across the block the boom
could not be pulled in.

"Chop away the jaws of the spanker boom," came Father's voice. No man could be spared to do anything for
McLean until the ship was safe. Nelson had found his
way back along the boom, holding on to the leachings of
the sail and was safe on deck now. With axes and crow-
bars the crew set about chopping away the spanker boom.
Better that it sink into the sea than push us on into the
path of the waterspout. I ran below and brought back a
big mug full to the brim with whiskey for McLean. We
had no chloroform or morphine on board, but the whiskey at least would help him to endure. In my innocence
I thought later it might knock him out completely. He
lay over the block, quiet except for a low monotonous
moaning. His breathing was very shallow. The veins in
his temples bulged in big throbbing cords. I poured the
entire mugful of whiskey down his throat. It might have
been water for any effect it had. The men hacking for

their lives at the jaws of the boom and the rigging had done their work. The boom crashed into the sea taking with it riggings and stanchions of the railing. But even free of the boom the ship went forward.

"We haven't got a chance," I heard Father mutter. He saw the waterspout was traveling at a course and speed sure to bring it close up across our bow.

Suddenly he shouted: "Joan, get my rifle!" I turned to run below for it and as I was disappearing down the companionway I heard his next command:

"Every man below the decks!" I could hear voices mumbling dissent, and Father's voice rose above the crew's as though he were beating them with his voice: "Get the hell below, you goddamned fools, or you won't have a Chinaman's chance!"

I brought up the rifle and handed it to him. He had lashed the wheel. "Throw a canvas over McLean," said Father through his teeth, "and then you get below!" Nelson had already got a big piece of canvas and he completely covered McLean with it. I ducked below without hesitation; I didn't know what was going to happen. I wondered if Father was going to use the rifle to kill McLean and mercifully end his suffering. I hadn't been below two minutes before I heard the report of his rifle! Then several reports followed in rapid succession and Father came running down the cabin himself, first closing the hatchdoor on the companionway.

"The shot busted it," he said simply.

We went to the lee portholes and looked out. Father said the shots from his rifle had started new currents in the air that broke the rhythm of the waterspout. Like a wounded beast the spout seemed to stagger and then collapse, dropping tons on tons of water, fish, and driftwood back to the sea. The spout when it collapsed was nearly half a mile away but the low heavy black clouds it came from were already over us and now they opened and emptied themselves just above the ship.

Did you ever see a cork under a waterfall? That was our ship beneath that downpour. Father had known what was coming and had saved the crew by forcing them below, for not one could have kept on the deck under the force of that bombardment with the ship pitching and wallowing in the conflicting currents and undertows like some blinded thing.

McLean covered with canvas and held fast by his crushed arm was the only living thing exposed.

I felt trapped down there below. The air was suffocating. The pressure of the humidity was so great that my pulses beat rapidly and I broke out in a cold sweat. Then in less than fifteen minutes the rain stopped abruptly, the clouds disappeared, the sun burst forth and the sea calmed as though nothing had happened.

"There won't be a whiff of wind now," Father said with disgust. With typical sailor fatalism he had dismissed the horror of the waterspout but he hadn't forgotten the trapped man above.

"We got to get that poor beggar out of that trap," he said, referring to McLean. I went on deck with Father to help him. We lifted the canvas off McLean's body. He lay cramped over in a doubled position, softly moaning.

"Can you stand it for another few minutes, old man?" Father asked.

He seemed to come from far away to answer: "Jesus,

Captain, take a pop at me with your rifle and finish it. I can't stand this!" His eyes were bulging in excruciating pain.

"Why, you goddamned bawling sissie, shut your face or I'll leave you squawking there all night!" Father yelled at him. The voice was terrible to hear but there were tears in Father's eyes. His bullying tone of voice was a trick to give McLean the guts to stand the ordeal he had to go through.

I was still shaking with fright from the terror of the waterspout as Father spoke to me and sent me below to get some iodine and his razor. When I brought them on deck to him he was leaning over, examining the steel couplets that had clamped McLean's arm.

"I'll have to cut your arm off, McLean. It's the only chance in hell you got to get out of this steel trap," he said.

McLean looked at Father, saw that he meant it, and that it was the only way to save him, and he forced a smile.

"Go ahead, Captain, but do it quick," he begged.

Father beckoned me to stand over McLean and keep his head lifted up. I got my arms under McLean's shoulders and heaved him up in a semi-sitting position. Bulgar and Swede held his legs. Another sailor brought a couple of buckets of sea water. Father twisted a tourniquet of rope around McLean's arm. Then he swabbed the arm just above the place where it was gripped by the steel, and cut in with his razor. McLean tried to watch him, but bracing his back with my leg, I put my arm across his eyes so he couldn't see himself being butchered. Bulgar and Swede jammed down on his legs to keep him from thrashing about. In about a minute Father had all the flesh sliced away from the bone. He leaned over to Swede and whispered. Swede went over to the rail and got a steel belaying pin. He raised it over McLean's arm. I saw Father nod and say "Now." And Swede brought the belaying pin down across the exposed bone of McLean's limb and broke the bone as clean as a hound's tooth.

"A bucket of sea water, quick," called Father. They poured two full buckets of water over the stub of McLean's arm. Ocean water is the best disinfectant against blood poisoning there is on a ship. I hated the job we had to do, for I could feel McLean trembling like one stricken with palsy. Blood sputtered out of his arm over the deck and over us. He began to laugh in a delirious frenzy. I kept hold of his head and four sailors gripped and held him so he couldn't move until Father had stitched up the shreds of flesh with catgut and a surgical needle. Then we carried him below and put him in my father's bunk. He had small chance of living, but Father kept that spark alive with big doses of whiskey every half hour. He left me to attend him, for he had duties on deck that were more serious. With the spanker boom gone, the rigging destroyed and no wind to steady us against the rising cross swells, there was danger of us "shaking our sticks (or masts) out."

For twenty-four hours the crew labored clearing the debris. They set up a makeshift spanker sail, "jury rig" it was called, in place of the boom. The horror we had been through was duly written down in our ship's log as follows:

"Thursday, P. M. 160 latitude, 32 longitude sighted waterspout. Shots from rifle broke it. Seaman J. McLean laid up unable to work. Crew busy clearing ship's deck."

Four months later McLean left the ship. There is no place on a ship for a one-armed sailor.

17

*Strip poker and female struck—which of course have nothing to do
with each other*

WHEN I was about sixteen, we took a trip to the Line
Islands to get a cargo of guano.

"What in the hell is the use of getting a ship full of
bird dirt?" I asked my father as we neared our destination.

He was balanced on the taffrail cleaning and oiling his
sextant when I approached him.

"Well, besides stinkin' worse than copra and bein' a
rotten cargo to carry through the heat of the tropics, it's
used for fertilizer and ammonia. Land folks ain't so particular what they use to make their food grow," he said.

I was keenly interested, for we were going to a part
of the South Seas that was unknown to me. So much has
been written about the colorful atmosphere of the South
Sea islands, but little has been said about the tragedy

that inhabits some of the desert rocks along the Equator known on the charts as the Line Islands.

No tropical foliage flourishes there, no sea blue lagoons, no fruits, flowers and long golden beaches enhance their nakedness. They are barren reefs, spewed up out of the sea by submarine volcanoes. As you approach them they look like snow-capped rocks with a fringe of white foam edging them from the breakers that crash against their cliffs. The screech of white gulls fills the air for miles around. The guano islands are the home of the sea fowl. There they lay their eggs in mating season. Millions of birds find those rock islands every year. The rocks are hardly fit for human habitation, yet a few men survive on them.

The French government owns the greatest number of those guano islands, and the income from them amounts to a small fortune every year.

I'll always remember my trip to those places for two reasons. First, it was on that voyage that I was introduced to the mysteries of strip poker and second, I saw a man so "female struck" that he swam a mile through a rough sea to get away from me.

The night before we sighted the Islands, Fred Nelson, Swede, Bulgar and Oleson were sitting in the lee scupper under the fo'c's'le head playing poker by the dim green glow of the starboard running light. I wasn't allowed forward of the mizzen mast unless my Father was with me, for that was the sacred domain of the crew. However, I went forward every time I got a chance, when Father wasn't looking. This particular night I waited until I heard him snoring on his settee before I tried it. Running along in the shadow of the sails on the leeward side I came upon the four men in the midst of the game.

They didn't pay the least attention to me. I stood by and watched them for about five minutes and then I butted in.

"Deal me a hand, will you?" I asked.

Swede looked up at me and then spat a big stream of amber juice over the rail. Oleson pretended he hadn't heard me, and Bulgar just scowled his disapproval of my presence. However, Fred Nelson was more sociable.

"Sure, Skipper, you can play next hand—but I advise you not to. This is strip poker we're playing."

For the first time I noticed certain oddities in the men's appearance. Swede had on nothing but his underdrawers. His shirt and dungarees were piled beside Oleson. Bulgar's pipe and leather belt were in front of Nelson. When the hand was finished Oleson handed over his clasp knife to Nelson also.

"See what it is? Now do you want to sit in?" asked Swede.

All I had on was a pair of overalls and a faded blue cotton blouse and me "as-is" underneath. With such a slim margin of safety to go on I probably would have withdrawn but for Nelson.

"Don't think you'd better try, Skipper," he said.

As usual, opposition made me stubborn.

"What's the reason I hadn't? Gimme cards!" and I plumped myself down.

Swede dealt me a hand. The cards were so dirty and worn and sticky with tobacco juice that it was hard to keep them separate in my hand.

"Ante up, Skipper," said Oleson.

I looked at my hand; I didn't even have a pair, but I wasn't going to let them bluff me out.

"One leg of my overalls," I piped up.

All except Swede laid down their cards.

"Ain't you takin' a chance?" said Nelson, looking at Swede's drawers.

"No more than she is," said Swede. "Raise you a whole bloomin' pair of pants," he bet, "and I better not lose!"

I could feel my face looked the picture of guilt.

"Two legs of my pants," was my come-back.

"Call you," grinned Swede. He showed a pair of jacks and a king, and I showed him a six, seven, a ten, and a queen and threespot.

"Hand over the wardrobe," he said.

I stared at him. There was nothing under my pants but me. And my pants now belonged to Swede.

"Hand 'em over, Skipper," he grinned.

Strip poker suddenly had become very unattractive.

"But—but—that's all I got on," I stuttered.

"What are you going to do, welsh?"

He stuck his chin out at me and his voice was the essence of contempt as he taunted:

" 'Tain't my fault if you force yourself into a strip poker game on just a pair of pants. What are you goin' to do?"

I don't know just what I would have done. Probably I would have taken off the overalls rather than fail to live up to the code of a true sailor, but Fred Nelson intervened.

"Skipper is a girl," he said, "and she don't take off nothin'."

"I'd 'a' give her my drawers if I'd lost," protested Swede.

"All right, I'll give you my pants," snapped Nelson.

"It's her pants I won!"

Nelson jumped to his feet.

"Do you take my pants or a punch in the guzzler?" he asked, very quiet, for that was the way he always was when he fought. He could whip any man on the ship except Father and they all knew it. Swede looked up at him and grinned.

"Gimme your pants, Nelson."

Nelson yanked off his pants, threw them at Swede and sat down beside me in his underdrawers.

"I'm through with this game and so are you," he said.

"But I want to win back your pants for you," I pleaded with him. Bulgar, the sly bully of the lot, spoke up. "I know how you can stay in the game without taking off anything, Skipper."

"How?"

He smiled craftily: "Pay your losses out of the slop chest."

The slop chest is the sea-going term applied to the Captain's ship store of gumboots, sailors' overalls, shirts, socks, sou'westers and shoes, and tobacco. Father invested some of his own money each trip to stock up with sup-plies and the expenditure was often a big sacrifice for him to make, for money was as scarce as hen's teeth. There was always something to eat up his profits: the ship had to go into drydock, then there were new canvas, ropes, and paint to be bought, bail for drunken sailors in foreign ports, to say nothing of cargo lost or damaged by storms. As a result Father kept a jealous eye on his slop chest. At sea when a sailor wanted to buy something the cost of the article was deducted from his pay at the end of the voyage.

This precious slop chest was stowed under the bunk in my cabin, and many a time in the night when a sailor had to get a sou'wester or warm socks or something because of sudden inclement weather, I would be routed from my bunk while Father dug under my mattress to get it for him. I had absolutely no sense of the economic value of things, for I never saw any money. Everything to me was an article of trade, and I would just as soon have given a fifteen dollar pair of rubber sea-boots in exchange for a pineapple as a three cent piece of calico. The idea that the things in the slop chest were Father's stores and important never occurred to me.

Naturally, therefore, I hailed Bulgar's suggestion with delight. Nelson wouldn't play but the others agreed I could stay in the game and pay my losses from the slop chest. But the next hand was no better for me. I got a pair of kings and I was so delighted with them that I grinned like a full moon as I bet. With one accord Swede, Oleson and Bulgar folded up their hands and wouldn't bet with me. I was licked either way—if I bluffed they called me, or if I had them they wouldn't come in, and in an hour of playing I lost three pairs of sea boots, one jersey sweater, ten pairs of socks, four shirts and eleven plugs of chewing tobacco.

"We want our winnings NOW!" they warned me, and I knew it wouldn't be healthy to hold out on them. Nelson made no further attempt to help. He was evidently disgusted with me.

I went aft to raid the slop chest, but I didn't trouble to

let Father know I was doing it. I lugged my losings forward and paid them to the sailors and sneaked back into my bunk, where I fell asleep with no twinge of conscience.

The next morning Swede came to the wheel in new dungarees, jersey and shoes, Bulgar went about cleaning brass in a brand new shirt and socks and Oleson had two plugs of tobacco sticking out of his back pants pocket. Swede's outfit caught Father's eye of suspicion and I held my breath for fear he'd start an investigation. When Bulgar walked right past him I knew I was sunk.

"Where in the hell did you guys get the new outfits—have you been stealing out of the slop chest?" Father inquired. His question made me wonder where I would be the most comfortable, up in the crosstrees of the foremast, or hid down in the lazarette underneath a bale of rope.

"No, sir," spoke up Bulgar. "We just had a bit of luck, sir."

Father went below and I knew he was going to take an inventory—so I went aloft and got very busy with a bucket of grease oiling down the topmast. I figured that if I was doing some useful ship's work when he caught me I would fare better. I hardly had time to get up to the crosstrees, swing into a bosun's chair and start swabbing grease on when I heard Father's voice booming out on the deck below:

"Call both watches on deck."

Keeping one eye on my grease rag and the other on the scene below I didn't miss a thing. Father made every man on board haul everything out of the fo'c's'le on the deck where he rummaged through everything looking for the things that had disappeared out of the slop chest.

Father yanked the shirt and sweater off Swede, and Bulgar and made them strip. I heard the sailors trying to explain that they had bought those articles of clothing ashore before sailing—and Father's answer to their alibis:

"Any louse that steals on the high seas ain't worth killin'," and he landed on Bulgar and knocked him head over heels. They took their medicine sailor-fashion without squealing and Father took their honest winnings back to his cabin—satisfied that he had taught his crew a lesson in honesty!

Swede and Oleson looked up at me in the rigging. I couldn't hear what they called me but I was sure it was no term of affection, so I decided to remain aloft. I don't know what they would have done to me but for Nelson and Stitches, who of course knew the story.

"Skipper is a kid and she never had a chance in a poker game with you robbers. It was honest stealin' on her part and dirty stealin' on yours and you got what was comin' to you," declared Stitches.

"And if you ain't satisfied and wants to get even, I'm glad to give you some more," added Nelson and then the cry from the look-out, "Land Ho!" ended the argument.

Our destination, the Line Islands, was in sight.

"You can't go ashore here, Joan. There's no tellin' what kind of riffraff is livin' on the island."

Father sailed the ship in as near as he dared without striking any sunken reefs. There was no sign of life that we could see, nothing except myriads of seagulls circling overhead.

"Where do the guano gatherers live?" I inquired.

"In a rocky cave, near the water. They can't live too high on the island because the fumes of the guano make poisonous gases."

I climbed the rigging of the mizzen mast so that I could get a better view of the island. I hung on with my toes to the ratlines to keep from falling off, for the swells and backwash from the shore were rolling the ship like a pendulum. I watched carefully for about twenty minutes, and then I saw a tiny black speck splashing in the water. As it came nearer, I saw it was the figure of a naked man, swimming out towards us. He was so burned by the sun that he was almost black.

"On deck," I called.

Father called back: "Hello?"

"Look at the native swimming out to us. He is just a quarter point off the stern," and I indicated with my hand to the spot where I saw the man swimming.

"He's comin' out to make a bargain with us for a load of guano," Father answered, megaphoning through his hands. I descended from my perch in the rigging by sliding hand over hand down a halyard. By the time I reached the poop deck, the "native" was within a hundred yards of us. We waved and called to him, and he raised a brown arm in answer. I was dressed in old faded overalls, and wore no blouse. My hair blew away from my face.

"What dialect does he speak?" I asked Father.

"One that you don't know, so for once you won't be able to hog the conversation—French!" I had never heard of a French dialect. I knew all the easy languages, —Samoan, Marquesan, Gilbertina, etc. but French was some savage language foreign to me. I wasn't going to be left out of the greetings, so I hollered as loud as I could: "Hello you!"

The native was right under the stern. At the sound of my voice he looked up. I smiled down at him. "Hello again to you," I said, and I smiled my best native trading smile. The native, who was a white Frenchman, stared up at me as if I were an apparition. He opened his lips as if to speak, his face flushed under its brown and he turned in the water as if struck by a bullet and swam back for the shore. Father called to him to stop. On he plunged back towards the island, and never once looked back.

"What in hell's the matter with him?" asked Father of no one in particular.

"Female struck," spoke up the mate. "These guys spend a lifetime on the islands alone and the sight of Joan with her exposed neck and shoulders and the curves around her hips set him nutty."

"What was he afraid of me for?" I wanted to know. "I didn't say anything except hello to him."

"There's a lot of things you got to learn about men, Skipper. I seen cases like this before. Sometimes the sight of a female drives them so crazy they kill themselves."

At that time I couldn't understand the mate's explanation. Why should a man be afraid of me? Father sent the mate and three sailors ashore to make the dicker for the cargo. When they returned the mate asked to speak to Father alone. It was obvious that he did not intend for me to know what he had to tell.

I was determined to know, however, so Father took me down into the cabin and explained:

"A man isn't complete without the love of a woman, some time in his life, Joan. A seagull can't fly with one wing, and neither can human beings really live alone by themselves and be whole. That man was convicted of a crime in France when he was a young boy about nineteen. The French Government, instead of sendin' him to Devil's Island for life, gave him the choice of workin' for a lifetime on this island. He lives worse than an animal in the foul atmosphere of bird manure. He eats nothin' but bird eggs and raw fish, and him just catchin' the sight of you made the man in him realize his aloneness."

I had never been conscious of my sex before that time. Father's words impressed me so deeply that I began to wonder about myself.

For three days we hove to while the crew made trips back and forth to the island in our boat with loads of guano. I had lost interest in the loading—I could only think of the derelict on that barren island.

18

A shanghaied crew and scurvy are poor bunkmates in a White Squall

THE following September we set sail for the Gilbert Islands with a load of trading articles to exchange for pearl shell. In our crew were just three old members: Bulgar, the Swede and Axel Oleson. The remaining men were shipped aboard at Sydney.

There was a labor strike on in Sydney at the time and to find a crew of non-union men willing to ship for the voyage was impossible. Father was up against it, but a crew he had to have and he was never a man to be balked by seeming impossibilities.

Now there is a widespread belief that "shanghaiing" as a common practice flourishes only in the stories of Jack London, Conrad and other writers of sea tales, but deep sea captains and sailors know better. So Father in his difficulty sought out a "sailors' runner," a ratty-faced little crimp familiar with the waterfront, and made his deal—five pounds a head for a crew.

"I'll want them aboard ship by five o'clock flood tide. I'm goin' to sail tonight without waitin' for any god-damned pilot and tugboat," he said to the crimp and returned to the vessel.

About four thirty that afternoon a launch sputtered alongside, and the mate and two sailors lowered a Jacob's ladder over the side. The man on the launch yelled up at them:

"Put over a cargo boom. These beggars won't come to until you hit the Equator."

I looked over the side and saw eight lumps of flesh, eight dead men, so it seemed, sprawled over the bottom of the launch like so many sacks of wet wheat. With every roll of the launch the bodies pitched from side to side in grotesque rhythm. Our men rigged up a cargo boom and tackle and the man on the launch slipped a running bow-line around one of the limp hunks of flesh.

"Take it away!" he grunted, and the sailors, with my help, pulled up the load.

It was a blond, husky Scandinavian. His body landed on the deck with a dull thud.

"Is he dead?"

The mate only looked at me contemptuously—as if anything could kill a Swede—and threw back the tackle for the next load of flesh. Over and over again they repeated that process until a row of eight bodies was on deck. The mate told me to call my father. I went below, almost sick, for I thought the men were dead. However, I was better trained in the code of the sea than to let anyone see I was affected by the sight of eight men laid out like corpses on the deck of the schooner.

I brought Father back with me. He reached down and

picked up the foot of the first man and let it drop back with a lifeless thud on the deck.

"He'll be a good man on a halyard," he said, and passed on to the next one. He was a dirty, uncouth-looking person so black with coal dust that he looked negroid.

"What a hell of a mess this is to soak me five pounds for," and he passed on to the next and the next until he had felt the muscles of each one. Satisfied that he had a good load of "beef" to pull on ropes in a storm or pump ship if a leak should spring, Father signalled the launch to cast off.

Turning to the mate, Father said:

"Take these so and so's forrard to the fo'c's'le and lock them in, then come aft and stand by. We'll sail out to-night anyway and sign those" (indicating the unconscious sailors) "on the Ship's Articles when they come out of it. You, Joan, take the wheel. I'll lend a hand to set enough sail to get out of here."

I was just short of sixteen at that time, husky and as strong as most men, and I felt myself to be as good a sailor as ever held a ship to a course. I went up on the poop deck to the helm, unleashed it and pulled with all my strength on its spokes.

"Hard over," called Father, and I slowly turned the big wheel.

"Hard over" means to turn the wheel completely around. Under my hands the wheel didn't turn as quickly as it should have, and Father let out a volley of curses at me that made the sky blue, but it also put vitality into me or scared some more strength into my arms, for I pulled the helm around as the wind caught the topsails and we glided out the Heads for the Gilbert Islands.

It was a hard week, that first one out, for the men were so drugged and beaten that they were slow in regaining consciousness. Three sailors, Father, the cook and myself navigated that big schooner, which in fair weather ordinarily required sixteen men to handle. I took the helm in the daytime, the sailors stood by the fore and main masts and the cook tended the jibs. Father slept in his clothes.

On the fourth day out we ran into the electrical storms off Lord Howe Island. Lord Howe is a barren island off the Australian coast, around which all the fury of the China Sea, Indian Ocean and South Pacific gathers. I'll never forget it—lightning so blinding and near that it made our eyes blur with blue shadows! Thunder which rattled so loud and so close that it reverberated on the deck!

And then, right in the midst of the thunderstorm the wind suddenly veered from southeast to north—northwest and we had to tack ship to keep from running aground.

The mate went aloft to free a tangled block from the mizzen topsail. He had reached the crosstrees and was straddled on them to balance himself as he freed the rope from the block. The lightning rods on the tops of the mast were alive with fire—they looked like huge gas jets aflame on the top of each spar. I was at the wheel, tied there by two ropes to keep from washing overboard in the seas that were sweeping over the poop deck. Father looked up to see if it was all clear aloft so he could let go the mizzen boom to tack over, when a streak of lightning made him cover his eyes with his hands to keep from being blinded. At the wheel I put my face down in my overalls' bib, and I guess the other men hid their eyes from the fiery onslaught of streak lightning, for not one of them saw just what happened. The mate aloft must have touched a ring bolt of steel on the mast and received the full shock! He dropped from the crosstrees to the deck, and his body was crushed into a mangled pulp by the fall. Before anyone could reach the spot where he fell a green sea swept across the deck and carried him overboard! It was too horrible—too gruesome! I crumbled inside. I don't know what would have happened to me if a sea hadn't washed over the poop and almost smothered me with water bringing me to.

The ship was "around" or tacked, and we were trying to hold her head up to the wind and keep her out of the belly of the swells to avoid capsizing. We couldn't possibly hold out much longer as the terrific strain had told on her strength. There seemed only one thing to be done as a last resort—revive the shanghaied sailors.

Father went into the fo'c's'le and attempted to rouse them. They only moaned and turned over and slept, or didn't move at all. It was four days later, exactly eight days from the time they were sent aboard ship, that they regained consciousness. The crimp had made a good job of them. He had first drugged them and then his gang beat them to lifelessness. Of the eight only two were sailors; the others were not worth their beans at sea as a crew. One was a waiter, another a truck driver, another a coal passer, another a cattle man and still another a hopeless dope fiend. The crimp had had a hard time finding heads to make up his blood money of five pounds apiece, so he had raided a waterfront saloon and made a wholesale slaughter of the available men he had found standing at the bar. All of them except the two sailors were seasick and cowardly of the storm.

With the mate dead and a bunch of landlubbers for a crew in one of the worst storms of the South Pacific, Father turned into a savage. The men had to sign on the Ship's Articles as seamen. It is maritime law that every man voluntarily sign his own name to the Articles, and in doing so, he becomes liable to obey the laws of the sea as dictated by the master of the ship. Once those men had put their signatures to the Articles, Father had them! They didn't want to sign, but when he invited them to sign or get off and walk, they wrote their names willingly.

Immediately after signing, the coal passer and cattle man made the mistake of refusing to go aloft to shift the topsails in the storm. Father took his revolver and pointed it at them.

"You dirty blank so and so's, you're sailors now. Get aloft and make fast those sails or you'll go over the side. Swimming isn't crowded around here," and he pointed to the seething ocean to windward. They went aloft.

The entire trip up through the islands was like that. Father was captain, mate and part of the crew and I was chief helmsman. The crew were unwilling prisoners, and they made life aboard a lively hell for us all.

As a result of poor seamanship and adverse winds, it took us ninety-three days to reach Papua. The ship was a mass of wreckage on deck—broken pieces of booms and rigging cluttered the scuppers. There was never any time during that trip that we had an uneventful day. Southerly busters, those vicious white squalls of the South

Seas, smacked our schooner and tossed us around like a cockleshell on the water. Then we reached the doldrums, that great area of deadly calms. Even in the calms there was no respite from the slapping and smashing of the rigging which was useless for sailing purposes and its battered condition. Ground swells from some distant storms shook the *Minnie A. Caine* until she wallowed like a drunken sailor.

Most people think the real dangers of the sea are storms, but to the deep sea sailor there is a terror greater than wind or sea which stalks in the wake of sailing ships long overdue—scurvy. Scurvy is caused by lack of fresh food, unhealthy water and heat on salt foods. The disease acts insidiously; the victim doesn't know he has it until terrific pains in his stomach make it impossible for him to eat anything. Then come headaches, blinding and maddening. The body appears dry and withered like the husk of a coconut. Fever and delirium follow, and in a short time, if medical relief or fresh food is not obtained —death!

Contrary to popular ideas and the maritime law of all countries, a ship's medicine chest usually contains nothing but Friar's Balsam, which is a sea-going iodine, salts, and blue ointment for vermin; none of which is a cure for scurvy.

Under the hardships of our voyage it was no wonder that we fell victim. For days at a time, while the decks were awash with swirling seas, the cook could prepare no meals. Time and again vainly he attempted to build a fire in the galley but no sooner would it begin to draw than the ship would list heavily to port, submerging the galley, cook and his pans in green seas. As a consequence

we lived on dried salt fish and lime juice. The shanghaied men couldn't even stomach that, and they were the
first to be stricken with scurvy. The coal passer had the
worst dose of all. His teeth dropped out one by one. His
body withered. He seemed at the point of death. The
cattleman, who was a sailor by circumstance, lost his
eyesight. None of us could sleep.

We put up the distress signal at the masthead and took
turns standing on lookout aloft for signs of another ship
or tramp steamer to bring us relief. That red flag
branded us as an outlaw, a crippled ship with a diseased,
dying crew aboard. All around us lay the monotonous
circle of horizon without a sign of life, except for an
occasional whale or school of flying fish. And so we wallowed on, expecting—waiting for death.

I was the last to get the scurvy. I suppose that was because I was the youngest and healthiest on board. When
it did hit me it was horrible. I felt I was dying from the
outside in. I would sit for hours and peel dead skin off
my body. When I look back on those days now I wonder
how we ever lived through it. Scurvy seems to make
savages of men at sea—they lose all sense of balance.
There is nowhere to turn for help—nothing to do but
suffer and wait for it to finish you. Only my father raved
at the bad luck:

"It's a goddamned shame. If I had anything but a
bunch of vomitin' landlubbers for a crew we'd be in
Honolulu now." He paced up and down the poop deck
from the rail to the binnacle and back. I crouched on the
hawser bit astern, picking dead skin off my arm.

"PORPOISE!!"

The cry brought us all to our feet. There, close to us on the windward side was a school of about twenty porpoises diving and snorting in the spray of the bowsprit.

"ALL HANDS ON DECK! MAN THE CAPSTAN! STAND BY THE HARPOON!"

Father rushed forward over the debris on deck. In less than five minutes every living man aboard was on the fo'c's'le head standing by to help land a porpoise.

A porpoise is a mammal and its meat is very like that of beef. If we could land one it would furnish fresh food for a week. Father stood down on the martingale under the jibboom, harpoon in hand. We waited praying for the porpoise to come near. The thin leader line from the harpoon was fastened to a three-quarter inch rope made fast to the capstan.

So eager was I to help land the porpoise that, not realizing what I was doing, I twisted the leader line of the harpoon around my hands. A big porpoise dived under the bow. Father hurled the harpoon. It struck the porpoise amidships and sunk in deep. The porpoise let out a squeal like a stuck pig and dived.

"Play out the leader line," called Father.

He was going to let the porpoise have plenty of rope for it couldn't get away with a steel harpoon through it, and sooner or later that harpoon would take its life. Six fathoms of line played out quickly, and then suddenly I was jerked with a terrific force to the edge of the fo'c's'le head. The porpoise, diving deep, had used up the slack, and I couldn't let go of the rope twisted around my hands. Slowly it slipped as the porpoise, with its two tons of weight, pulled, and the slipped rope burned inches into my hands, cutting, burning the flesh off down to the bone. I was being dragged overboard with only my own strength against that of the maddened, dying porpoise.

Two sailors grabbed me, trying to hold me back. They nearly pulled my arms from their sockets, but the porpoise took us all closer and closer to the edge of the low rail. Father looked up from the martingale and saw what was happening. He reached out, grabbed the taut leader line, and with a jerk using all his strength, managed to slack it for a moment. The porpoise, under the water, changed its course, turning back underneath the keel. That saved my life. The leader line caught in the hawse hole and held until one of the men cut the line free. The porpoise was gone, taking that harpoon with it.

The line was twisted and cut into my hands so deeply that Father had to pull it out. He looked at the raw flesh hanging on the bone, and without wasting words, dashed for the galley. In a minute he was back with a handful of wet salt.

"Hold out your hands."

I held them out and he spread that wet salt on the deep burns. The pain was so great I thought I couldn't stand it. I suppose now if that happened to me I would cry or moan or faint, but then I took it like a sailor. I cursed until the air was blue, and cursing that way held back the tears, for I would rather have been drawn and quartered than have let a sailor see me bawl—even though those sailors were seasick, shanghaied landlubbers.

The men set about to harpoon another porpoise and got one on deck within an hour. As they hoisted it aboard it opened its long snout and squealed and hollered. Father shot it several times, then chopped its head off with an ax.

The men were like vultures, hovering around for the first taste of its blood to relieve their fevered throats. The Jap cook snatched the ax from Father's hand and licked the raw blood off it. Then Father hacked off a piece of blubber and meat for each-sailor. He gave me a piece of its bloody liver and the tragedy then was not my burned hands, but that I couldn't hold anything in them to eat. I lay down on the fo'c's'le head and lapped up the blood, chewing at the liver like a dog.

That fresh blood saved our lives. Five days later we dropped anchor in Papua, a "plague ship" manned by semi-delirious men.

It is such things as this that make me wonder why land folks think being the daughter of a sea captain is so romantic.

19

The Dance of the Virgins on Atafu

AT Papua we all put in to the marine hospital for treatment. One of the most dangerous things to do after starvation and scurvy is to eat, but it is almost impossible to keep from gorging oneself on food at the first opportunity. I traded a plug of tobacco with a native for a dozen bananas and I ate ten of them. The result was that my stomach swelled and I took on the proportions of a fat turtle in pain.

We were in port for a month, while the ship was being repaired and the sailors were recovering. If Father could have found any sailors at Papua he would have shipped them in a minute, but they are scarce in that part of the world, and beachcombers or halfbreed natives were the only crew he could assemble as he struck out once more from Papua to the Union Group of Islands, which are situated about twenty-eight degrees south of the Equator and one-hundred sixty-seven longitude west.

All of the hardship of the trip thus far was paid for as far as I was concerned when we made Atafu. This is the largest island of the Union Group, and at that it is only three miles long by half a mile wide. It is atoll shaped, around a blue lagoon of clear water. Atafu is what is known as one of the coral islands, for its base is pale pink coral. The island rises about three feet above sea level, and is covered with thick tropical foliage. The palms are thirty to forty feet high, and the underbrush is a tangled jungle of tropic vines.

Breadfruit trees, coconuts, yarrow root, banana and plantain palms, blossoming hibiscus flowers, poisonous wild peas, giant morning-glory vines and little native berry plants grow there in such profusion that as you approach the southeast side of the island it looks like a solidly woven mat of green and white. The beauty of Atafu is distinct from other South Sea islands. The sand on its horse-shoe beach is an orange gold, the coral jutting out under the white spray of the surf a delicate pink against the transparent green sea. Then within almost a stone's throw from the beach inland lies the opalescent, bottomless lagoon. The natives say that at the bottom of the lagoon, which is so deep it has never been fathomed, in the "Sunset Land": their heaven. They will tell you in all earnestness that that lagoon reaches to the other side of the earth where the sunsets are painted, and as natives worship beauty that far away the place at the pit of the lagoon is to them the "hereafter."

The village which nestles on the edge of the jungle is composed of queer little three-cornered houses of coconut fibre matting. These houses are movable, and if the wind veers around or rain comes, the native husband

turns his hut around to keep out the storm. The huts are
only about four by six feet, and can be lifted by one man
—it is no uncommon sight to sail up to Atafu and find
the whole village gone. Not a sign of a hut or a living
thing anywhere. That happens in the hurricane months,
which are June and July in the tropics. The island is so
low to sea level, that the giant breakers whipped up by
a hurricane wash far upshore, even to the edge of the
lagoon. The natives spend six months a year preparing
for their winter. On the lee of the island, they dig caves
and barricade them with twigs and woven palm leaves
to shut out the wind. The women dry fruit and fish and
bury it in the bottom of the cave for provision during
the two months of hiding. One of the rarest delicacies
they preserve is sun-dried plantains. These plantains are
a species of banana. They let the intense heat of the sun
crystallize them to sugar, then wrap them in damp leaves
of morning-glory plants. The plantain thus wrapped
turns to a sugary wine. They are wrapped up in little
bundles that look like a Spanish tamale. I knew of some
travellers who were touring the South Seas and their
charts gave an accurate position of the native villages
on each island in that group. When they returned to Australia they reported that they had found no sign of life.
That was because they arrived there during hurricane
time. I once asked a native Chief if his people didn't
grow restless during the two months they were buried
alive on the island, and he said "No, they all get very
no-doing," which means drunk. The native men take
coconuts and punch holes in the nut to let air get to the
milk. Then they stop it up and let it ferment, thus brewing
a liquor that is more deadly than any pre-Volstead drink

ever conceived. I saw one of our sailors take a couple of drinks of coconut wine, and topple over me as if he had been hit on the head with a belaying pin, so I never pitied those natives who were forced by the elements to lie in a cave and suck wine while the sailors at sea had to struggle to keep a ship afloat.

The trip to Atafu was uneventful, except for Father's vocabulary of profanity which he developed in finding expletives to describe his landlubber crew's seamanship.

About five o'clock of the night of October 19th, we hove to off Atafu. There is no anchorage there so we had to drop extra sail and keep the ship up in the wind. The natives had evidently sighted us long before we saw Atafu, for the beach was a swarming mass of black men, wildly gesticulating to us.

Father called to me, "You get your trading stuff on the poop deck, Joan, we want to get a chance to trade before you cheat them out of their breech clouts." I have always been able to get more from the natives by trading than any six sailors, and Father said I must be cheating! My particular store of goods to trade consisted of pieces of tinfoil off chewing gum and tobacco which I had begged from the sailors, boxes of matches, ivory soap, and red calico. The natives were crazy to get the tinfoil. They rolled it into little knobs and put it on their bushy hair like jewels. The matches were my next best bet for a good trade. I would give them two matches for a Panama hat or a handful of bird of paradise feathers. Ivory soap was especially valuable in trading. The old natives would give me a rare mat, or a box of sandalwood inlaid with raw pearl for a cake of it. No, they didn't want the soap to wash in; they ate it for dessert! The red calico was for the women. From them I would coax a ring of tortoise-shell inlaid with blue mother-of-pearl, or fans painted on palm leaves with berry juices.

"Drop over a Jacob's ladder," called Father as four heavily laden outrigger canoes shot out toward us. These outriggers are so built that they will not capsize in a surf, and they were overflowing with bunches of bananas, breadfruit, dried fish, and wild chickens, about the size of pigeons. Years before some whaling captain must have given them some chickens and they interbred them so much that they degenerated until their offspring became as small as pigeons. They live wild in the trees and the natives sneak up on them at night and catch them.

"Ora-ai," shouted a large native in the bow of the first canoe. That meant "Friendly we come as friends." The large man was none other than Rara-mongai, the native Chief of Atafu. Rara-mongai was the largest man on the island and by virtue of his stature he was king. When he died the next biggest man would succeed him. Rara-mongai was all dressed up for the gala occasion of the "white man's ship with wings" arrival. The natives see about two ships a year and it is a big event when one will stop and trade with them. As that native Chief climbed up the Jacob's ladder loaded down with strings of rare shells, he was the queerest looking live thing I had ever seen. His fuzzy hair was turning grey, which seemed to accentuate his black skin. He wore an old full-dress coat, a woman's muslin petticoat, (it looked like the cast-off of some sea captain's wife) which ended above his knees, and a string of jewelry around his waist. His jewelry was rusty hardware that had washed ashore from some passing ships. A tomato can jangled amidships, ring bolts of iron came next to that, and an old colander and a can opener. The chief wore them as ornaments, for to him they were strange, weird, unheard-of things, those bits of sea-washed, rusty hardware.

Rara-mongai stepped forward and placed a string of shells around my neck, and then one around Father's. That was a sign of friendly welcome, too. Father made the sign of friendship back to him and we waved to the blacks in the canoes to come aboard. They scrambled up the side of the ship like screaming monkeys. Their bronze bodies were naked except for a protecting breech clout. In a flash they had unloaded their canoes and were chattering wildly for bargains. In the last canoe, unnoticed apparently, were two women. They were so fat they weighed the canoe down astern. The youngest of them was the Chief's daughter, "Good," and the other woman was her nurse.

"Come on aboard," I called to them, in English, forgetting in my excitement to speak their dialect. They just held on to the edge of the canoe and grinned. My pantomime convinced them I wanted them, so they climbed aboard, but with great difficulty. Father and the sailors were engaged on deck trading, so I sneaked the women down to the cabin of the ship. I asked them if they wanted something to eat; they said they did, so I called the cabin-boy and told him I would eat my supper then. Those two native women never in their lives had been inside a room without fresh air, and that, combined with the rolling of the ship, made them seasick. They were game, though, to see it through. I was watching them to see what they would do just as they were curiously watching me. They sat at the table when the food was served. First came soup. I watched them to see if they knew what to do with it. They didn't, but they watched me, then followed my every movement and ate the soup. They had never tasted any food in their lives except native fruits and fish, so the expression on their faces at onion soup was one of wonderment. All during the meal they laughed and gurgled, and stared at me. Suddenly Good and her nurse heard a commotion up on deck and I told them to wait a minute and I would be back. The noise I found there was the natives shoving off for the island. The Chief said to Father:

"You come, Chief of white-ship-with-wings and I make fun for you." Father wasn't very anxious to go ashore to have natives "make fun," or dance for him.

"Can I go?" I asked, fearing he would forbid me to be out of his sight for an hour.

"All right, you can go ashore and help those two blankety-blank landlubbers fill the kegs with fresh water."

I turned and disappeared down the companionway before he could take back his promise. There I found Good and her nurse just finishing the contents of the swill barrel. While I was gone they had prowled into the pantry, thought the garbage was part of the strange new food and ate every mouthful of it. I had to get three natives and Father to carry them up to the deck and fresh air.

Some of the natives at the signal from the Chief to return to the island, jumped overboard, their breech clouts bulging with their trades, the others pulled back in the outriggers. I started to get in the outrigger with Good but Father caught me by the seat of my pants, just as I was going over the side.

"Hey you, you go ashore in the dinghy with the crew. Bring back two barrels of fresh drinking water, and when you get them filled come smack back here to the ship."

"Yes sir," I answered, only too eager to obey. Bulgar and the Swede, the waiter and the truck driver and myself put off with the two barrels. It is one thing to land an outrigger canoe through a surf, and quite another to get a clumsy ship's boat with two water kegs and four people in it ashore. Swede sculled, and I stood in the bow directing him through the channel, for I could see over the reef. A long sinuous green comber sneaked up on us and lifted us high in the air, then let us down with a smack in the surf. We got by that, but another came before we got righted out of the swell, and it took boat, landlubbers, sailors, water kegs and me, and sent us flying toward the beach smothered in foam. I dodged a water barrel and landed without a scratch on the beach, but the boat was lost. It broke up into splinters. The water barrels washed ashore. I don't think I was as sorry as I should have been about losing the boat, for without it Father couldn't get ashore, and we couldn't get back to the ship. I didn't care particularly, because I wanted to explore the island. Before I had shaken the water off myself I was surrounded by a dozen or more boys, about twenty years old. They formed a circle around me, and were laughing. Finally, with a great show of bravado, one of them dashed up to me and touched the white skin on my legs, whereupon all the others shouted and cheered. I was the first white girl they had ever seen and they wanted to know how white skin felt under their dusky fingers.

With a guard of them we were taken to the center of the village to the Chief. That kindly old man was very much concerned over our accident. However, Good was not concerned, sulked on the floor of the hut, and would have nothing to do with me. I think she credited me with being responsible for the pains in her stomach from her meal of garbage. However, I was undaunted—I was ashore once more. I had my bare feet on real land again so didn't care about anything else.

"Chief, where is the water for our barrels?" I asked. Instead of summoning a servant to take me to the native reservoir, he himself took me by the hand and led me down a path through the jungle. Hand in hand we walked, and the sailors followed behind carrying the two barrels and cursing at the stickers in the jungle that were cutting their bare feet.

In native dialect Rara-mongai said to me:

"Over there, in the hollowed-out heart of the palm trees we save water. When it rains, water goes inside the palm trunk. Save it for dry months."

He pulled some green leaves away from a row of chopped off banana palm trunks, and there, inside of each, were trunkfuls of cool fresh water. I tasted it, and it had the tang of palm pitch in it, which made it the more refreshing. Carefully, using coconuts and tortoise-shells for dippers, he helped us fill the two barrels.

"Tonight when moon comes up full, dance of Virgins in the village. You stay and see all by my side. Your friends (meaning the sailors) they stay too and see Virgin dance."

"Virgins? Sure I'll stay," piped up Bulgar.

"What is the Dance of the Virgins?" I asked.

"Every year young girl ready to marry. Must choose mate at Virgin Dance. Then become good wife because she pick husband alone."

I was so anxious to stay and see the dance that I forgot all about returning to the ship. I asked Swede, as he was the oldest sailor and therefore had the most authority over the others, if he wanted to stay.

"Hell yes, Skipper, any time any virgins dance that's where you'll find me." As long as' he had expressed a willingness to stay also I saw no occasion to hurry back aboard ship, so we followed the Chief to the village. The sun had set, and the moon was just beginning to dip out of the horizon. I sat at the Chief's feet, and the men stood behind him and watched the festival begin.

Once a year it is the custom in Atafu to have a marrying festival, which is celebrated by the Dance of the Virgins. An Atafu girl is ready to marry when she is ten or eleven years old, and she alone has the choice of her husband. No man can woo her until she has given him the sign that she has chosen him. The marriage festival is the biggest event of the year. The little girls shine their gold brown bodies with coconut oils. Instead of preparing lavish wardrobes they make their skins shine like burnished gold. Over their left ear, snugly tucked in their thick hair to assure its not falling out during the dance, is a white lotus or hibiscus flower. The white hibiscus is a flower sacred to virgins, and when they place one on the left ear it is the sign that they are ready to take a mate.

The moon rising on the set day of the festival is the signal for the dance to begin. All the young men who are going to take a wife, or rather who desire a wife, line up on the left side of the Chief, and stand with folded arms and watch the dance. The folded arms are a sign of "must not touch, but only look" until the dance is over. Slowly and almost inaudibly at first, then gradually becoming louder and more wild and barbaric, it burst into a thrilling savage rhythm. The tom-tom is the tribe's only musical instrument. They have never heard of the ukulele or guitar. I have found out since that the ukulele was introduced into the Hawaiian Islands by a boy from Harvard!

As the beating of the tom-toms swelled, the virgins, nine in all, started their dance—there in our presence they unfolded the sacred rite of virginity crying for a mate. Every movement of their muscles has a meaning, and it is foreign to the meaning that the civilized world has put upon it. The Chief, on seeing the sailors' spellbound gaze, said:

"On your far-away island United States men pay women many gifts to make bad our dance." I hotly denied that accusation. The hula-hula, which is always associated with the South Seas, is a cheap imitation of the real thing, but at that time I had never heard of it.

The writhing of their abdomens was symbolic of calling upon the fires of the earth to burn their wombs clean for the coming of a manchild to make their tribe strong. Their waving arms called on the sea to bring them ships loaded with treasure, and on the winds to bring long life to their body, so that their loved one would enjoy them long. As the music swelled their dance became more uncontrolled; they seemed to be spirits inside of native bodies trying to express a hunger for mating.

Suddenly the music stopped, the girls threw themselves

on the ground singing a triumphant song, but the left hand of each was cupped over the lotus flower to keep it from the ground.

Rara-mongai rose from his throne and walked to the middle of the clearing where the girls lay. A hush fell, as he solemnly spoke:

"To you who are looking for a wife, I speak. The strongest men alone can have maidens. Here in moonlight on festival night, each man step forward and show what strength of body he has that the maidens may choose the greatest of you."

A native man's way of wooing is to show off in front of his bride to be, physically. He tries to outdo his rivals by excelling in physical strength, such as husking a coconut with his teeth, stabbing a wild boar, diving and killing a shark single-handed. Instead of protesting their love in so many words they believe in action, and by displaying physical supremacy, they think to impress the women that they are the masters. At the Chief's words about twenty young natives stepped forward eagerly. The truck driver and Swede made a dive for the center of the clearing too.

"Say, Chief," spoke up Swede, "I'm stronger than any of these young pups, and I'll take that little girl with the nice fat figger." Swede was so pleased with himself that he didn't notice the anger in Rara-mongai's face. He spoke harshly in his dialect:

"Maidens choose husband. No white man touch my people."

To Swede, the dance had just been a good show, and sailor-fashion he was entering into the spirit of it, not realizing he was violating the most sacred rite of Atafu.

By intervening I gained the favor of the Chief once more. The girl that Swede had pointed out never took her eyes off him during the rest of the ceremony. A white man wanted her, and she wouldn't make any effort to attract her own native kind. Any white man in the South Seas who is healthy looking and strong, can win a native woman away from any native or chief.

For two hours while the rest of the villagers feasted, the native men wooed the virgins by showing off athletically. Not one word is spoken, the whole story of their desire is in pantomime. When the moon reached the center of the sky, the Chief called for silence. According to the custom of the tribe he told the girls that now they must choose a man, by taking the lotus from their left ear and placing it on the right ear of the chosen one. I looked at the faces of the twenty young men who stood in a row hoping to be selected. As the girls walked up slowly with the lotus blossoms in their outstretched hands toward them, fear and triumph flashed down the line. Three girls went to one young buck and gave him their lotus, another man received two flowers, and the others one. Those that were passed up by the girls once more folded their arms in to their bodies.

"Huh," grunted Swede contemptuously, in my ear, "if those birds just fold their arms and lay down on the job no wonder the janes didn't pick 'em."

The Chief walked to the three girls who had picked one man, and did a Solomon. He handed the man to the girl who had reached him first. Primitive law, administered swiftly and without question. A couple stood before the Chief. With his tortoise-shell emblem of state he touched the girl and the man on the head, the native sign of wedlock. To the woman he said:

"By choosing this man you now become nothing. He is the stronger. If any man touch you after this wedlock the man shall be punished, for you have no right or privilege to say what shall be done with your body. If your husband gives privilege of your body to man he must be paid for it. If man take you without your husband's willingness, that man shall be sent to the coral reef to scrape the salt that dries there from the surf. There he shall stay until he is again like a child (until madness seizes him) and then he shall fall in the sea."

The native man turned to the girl, she lifted her bare shoulder to his lips, and he bit her until her blood came. The Chief went on:

"Woman's blood in husband's body make you one always."

Then to the man, the Chief admonished: "Every girl come now and touch her body to your body. If you do not desire them when they touch you, your choice of wife is good. You have woman good for you."

He beckoned to a group of the youngest and prettiest girls in the village. One by one they sidled up to the groom and in the most alluring and sensuous manner, they let their bodies caress his. The groom stood with his eyes averted, unmoved. It was a triumph over temptation, and that was the signal for the tom-toms to burst into an exotic rhythm, as the married pair walked hand in hand down to the lagoon. There is a tribal custom on Atafu that every newly married couple walk hand in hand up to their necks in the waters of the lagoon, they cleanse themselves together, and when they have done that, their marriage is consummated before the eyes of all.

When the last couple was married, the festival was over, and dancing, singing and feasting lasted long into the night. I had forgotten all about time, the water barrels and Father's order to come right back to the ship. By the position of the moon I guessed it was about four A. M. A frightened cry from a native running up from the beach broke in on the revelry. Wildly he pointed to the ship off shore. The truck driver who never had much to say at any time laconically observed:

"The Old Man's sending up flares from the vessel. Guess he thinks a cannibal swallowed you whole."

I was in for it and I knew it. I could feel my hind part tingling in anticipation of what was going to happen when Father got his hands on me.

"Let's beat it back to the ship, Swede. There won't be a barnacle left on my bottom when Father catches me."

"Yeh? Well, what's your hurry, how you going to get the water barrels back?"

I knew I'd catch hell for staying ashore, but to come back minus a life boat and no fresh water was suicide.

"Say, Chief, will you lend me an outrigger and a couple of men to bring it back, so I can get back to the ship?"

The Chief smiled, and said:

"White girl always ora-aii on Atafu. I help you go, but sorry. Some day come back again?"

I would have promised that Chief anything just to get off the island. He gave us an outrigger and we shoved out for the schooner. I saw the red distress flares from the ship light up the sky—Father was in earnest, and the moon was so bright I could plainly see the hull of the ship from the beach. Without much difficulty we got beyond the surf and were soon alongside. I let the sailors go aboard first. They threw over a bowline and hauled the water kegs on deck. Father was at the Jacob's ladder leaning over the side, smoking his pipe. The smoke was coming out of it in fast jerks, and I needed no barometer to tell me a storm was coming.

Leisurely I climbed the rope ladder, for I was in no hurry to get aboard. Halfway up Father called:

"Where in hell is the dinghy?"

"I was going to explain to you about that, Father. We were trying to ride the surf and we capsized and. . . ."

I got no further. Father had me by the neck and seat of the pants, hurrying me up to the poop.

"I can understand these so and so landlubbers upsettin' a boat, but you're my daughter and I won't believe any yarn like you losin' control of a dinghy."

Along about dawn I was comfortable enough to sit down without too great pain! We were sailing along under full canvas, and Father, evidently content that I could get into no further deviltry, had turned in for a nap.

Swede and the sailors were sitting on the hatch near the mizzen mast. From my place at the wheel I heard Swede saying:

"Yeh, I coulda had any one of those dames, they was crazy about me; that fat little nigger wench is just busted-hearted to see me leave."

And it was me that got a licking!

I was never to forget that experience on Atafu. I thought that everybody in the world was married according to native custom. I thought that some day I, too, would be taken to a dance where I could pick out my mate.

The days that followed our departure from Atafu became dull and monotonous. The sound of the tom-toms and the vision of the native girls abandoning themselves in a dance, was constantly before me. I hadn't even had a licking for almost a week and the calm atmosphere was too much for me. I would have to start something if nothing was going to happen of its own accord. I started a cockroach war. I caught two big cockroaches and tied their bodies together with pieces of thread. Then I went around to the sailors and took bets on them. I drew a line on the deck and put a roach on either side of it. The one that pulled the other over the line won. I bet two plugs of tobacco and one of Father's undershirts on the fattest cockroach, but the ship took a list to leeward just as he started to pull hard, and the other cockroach won and I lost. In novels of the sea the Captain's daughter is frequently pictured as occupying herself with lovely feminine pastimes, but cockroaches, rats, or bedbug hunts were more fascinating to me. But even in the trade winds those games tired me. I wanted action.

One afternoon, finding nothing more exciting to do, and when I was sure Father was asleep, I started on my own Dance of the Virgins. I didn't have anything I could use for a lotus flower except a pair of dried flying-fish wings. I put them behind my left ear as I had seen the native girls do. I wasn't sure just which one of the sailors on watch I would give that flower to, but that was to come later anyway.

Swede was at the wheel. I whispered to him:

"Will you go forward and get me a can full of grease from the cook? I'll take the wheel for you." He was glad of any excuse to get away, so he consented. He brought back a can of salt pork dripping from the galley.

"What are you goin' to do with that stuff?" he asked.

"Don't talk so loud, Swede. I'm goin' to do that Virgin Dance the way we saw them do it on Atafu."

"Jeeze," he said.

I went down on the main deck near the mizzenmast and began greasing my body. I took off my overalls, and gave my body a glorious shine that would rival any I saw on the island, and started the dance. I pounded on a rain barrel for a tom-tom. Every sailor on deck beat it just as I got going. They had seen Father's head appearing out of the companionway, but I hadn't. The next thing I knew Father grabbed me but my body was so slippery he couldn't keep a hold on me.

"What the hell are you doing?" he yelled.

"Just dancing the way the girls danced for us on Atafu," I answered, and I ran aft and locked myself in the flag locker.

Father followed me, but couldn't unlock the door. "I'll knock hell out of you when I lay hands on you," he promised. I had no intention of ever coming out of that flag locker. Hours later I heard the dinner-bell ring. I was greasy and hot and hungry, but I thought better than to venture out. At dusk I heard a low whistle outside the porthole. I looked out and saw a piece of bread dangling there on a piece of string. The Jap cook had taken my side, and smuggled me some supper. The next morning I unlocked the door and looked around for Father. He was busy on his chart. I stood by him wrapped up in a flag. I thought I might as well get the licking over with so he could go on with his work. However, he didn't even speak. He reached up to his book shelf and took down an illustrated copy of Dante's Inferno, and opened it to the illustrations of women burning in fire in hell. I was cured. I would never be a dancer!

20

A Love Story—which is an end and not a beginning

"THEM'S Portuguese Men-o-war, Skipper," explained Stitches when I asked him what the floating, transparent little blue things were that I saw glistening in the sunlight on the surface of the sea.

"Yep, them little tri-cornered sails on them looks like old Portuguese ships of war, that's where they gets their name."

"Are they fish?" I asked.

"Kind of. They is barnacles in the making. When they catch fast to the bottom of a ship with their little blue threads of trailing anchor lines they petrify into shell and that is how barnacles grow."

I marveled that the little inch high jelly ships could ever turn into the curse of seamen—barnacles! There was a fleet of thousands of them before my eyes.

"As long as they keep moving they is all right, but they are like some cussed folks ashore who, when they

stick on to someone else, turn into a damned nuisance,"
Stitches concluded. It was another lesson I learned from
the sea. Only a few days before we had passed through
a floating mass of porous-looking petrified lava—the
spewed up evidence of an undersea volcano in erup-
tion. There was so much of it that it gave the appearance
of floating land.

"Shore folks call that pumice stone and they grind it
up to make tooth paste," Stitches had said. Why did shore
people make everything so difficult for themselves? I
used salt to brush my teeth with, not lava from deep sea
volcanoes.

"It appears like you was usin' up a lot of wind ask-
in' questions with your mouth—and your mind is
a-headin' off to leeward on another tack. Ever since
you seen that love dance on Atafu you been moonin'
around."

Stitches' words struck home. The beauty of the dance,
the thrill of seeing the native girls choose their mates,
and the expression of longing on the native men's faces
to possess the girls haunted me. No matter how I tried I
couldn't drive the memory from my mind. I pretended
to be interested in ship work, but really just one problem
absorbed my mind. I wanted to mean everything to some
one person—I wanted to be wanted. My loneliness on
shipboard was accentuated after I saw the marriage
dance on Atafu. Where would I find a mate? I didn't
have any lotus to wear to make any man choose me. In
fact none of the men on board seemed to have the slightest idea of the thoughts constantly in my mind—I was
just a nuisance, and no one of them ever showed an in-
clination to offer himself. I probably never would be

taken to a dance where I could pick out my man. Then
the thought came: the girls on the island could choose
only from the men they knew and the dance was merely
a method of selection. After all, getting the man was
the important thing and if the native girls had an island
full of men to pick from—I had a shipload, so I became
encouraged.

I would find my man on board the ship and so I began to look over the crew. First, of course, there was
Stitches. I loved him but not as a prospective mate. He
looked so much like a wise old turtle, and if I spoke to
Stitches about my plan he'd go to Father and I'd get a
mug full of salts or a rope's end on the back of my lap
to clear away "crazy fancies." The rope's end never
really hurt—my body was too tough. But of late my ideas
with regard to lickings had changed. They made me furi-
ous. I was getting too old to be treated as a child. That's
what I thought. But what I thought made no difference
to Father. It was the rope's end or the salts, clear to the
last day we were on the ship.

So it was plain Stitches would not do.

There were the two mates. Strange, but all the time I
was on the ship we never had a mate I really liked. I
passed them over. There were just four of our old men
on board now, Stitches, Swede, Bulgar and Nelson; the
rest of the crew to me were just sailors, new men who
meant nothing.

I considered Swede again. He was big and strong but
he could never stand the test of beautiful girls caressing
him without being tempted. Bulgar, well, he was too
much of a bully.

I was sitting on the main hatch helping the watch

splice ropes into a bumper when the first really concrete idea came to startle me. Nelson was splicing a rope opposite me. Why hadn't I thought about him? Somehow he was the last one I ever wanted to think about, yet he measured up finer than any of the crew. He could spit a curve, he had hair on his chest. Just looking at him at that moment made me feel funny. I got hot and cold all at once, and my fingers tangled the rope splice.

"Aw, he ain't the one," I declared to myself, and I got up and left the hatch. I climbed up to the crosstrees. The more I thought up there at the masthead the more tangled my mind came. Nelson kept coming in my thoughts, but I'd shove him out. That night I stayed on deck very late. The moon was out, and the soft air from the trade winds barely kept the sails full. At four bells, Nelson came to take his trick at the wheel. He didn't seem to notice me lying in the belly of the spanker sail. He just kept his eyes on the topsails and on the compass. I didn't dare speak to him as long as Father stayed on deck, but about eleven o'clock Father went below to turn in. The mate was pacing his beat down on the main deck so my way was clear. There is a maritime law that prohibits anyone talking with the man at the helm so I had to do it very quietly.

"Nelson!" I whispered. He looked up to where I was lying.

"Huh?"

"Are you like all sailors? Are you in love with the curves of the sails too?" He was startled by my sudden question, but after a moment he said:

"Hell no! I ain't in love with no skirt, imaginary or real."

I couldn't think of any answer to that so I kept quiet. He looked at me so steadily I thought he'd let the ship get off her course. After several minutes of silence he said in a voice that sounded as if he was talking about a cargo of copra:

"Skipper, you know you're a pretty kid."

I thought he was being sarcastic. I jumped off the sail and ran below where I threw myself on my bunk and cried. I hated him for making fun of me. Hadn't my father told me I was ugly? Why was Nelson just rubbing it in? I hated him, and for hours I lay awake wishing the ship would sink and he would be the first one to drown. But in spite of everything, the next day I found myself forgiving him. It was Sunday and we had the inevitable duff cake for dessert. Instead of eating my piece I stowed it away in my overall's pocket to give to him, for the fo'c's'le didn't rate desserts. He stood his trick at the wheel that afternoon from two to four. He didn't even look at me when I came on deck, but I walked past the wheel and stuffed my hunk of precious cake in his hand. He took it and began to eat it. I sat on the skylight and watched each swallow go down while my mouth watered for just a taste of the dessert I took joy in sacrificing for him.

"This is good grub," he said between mouthfuls. The last bite went into his mouth but a corner of it fell to the deck. Oh, if he wouldn't see it I'd wait until he left the wheel and pick it up and eat it myself! I stood guard from my perch on the skylight over that piece on the deck. When Oleson came to relieve him, Nelson's big bare foot stepped on the piece of cake by accident and ground it into some tobacco juice on the deck!

Fred Nelson was a Dane. He had yellow hair and
light blue eyes. He was about thirty years old, and as
strong as three average men. He was the only man I had
ever seen that had gold hairs on his chest—and those
curly ones. He was different from the rest of the crew.
He wouldn't let me play strip poker. When he looked
at me he made me wish I didn't wear overalls. I imagined
there was an expression in his eyes of hunger when he
looked at me, yet he avoided speaking to me whenever
he could. He had been on the ship for six years and never
in all that time did he show fear in a storm or shirk the
hardest job.

I did everything that I could to worship at his feet,
without letting him know of it. One hot night, about a
week after the duff cake disappointment, I was sleeping
in the lifeboat which was hung over the stern. I awoke
and through half-closed eyes I saw Nelson hacking a curl
of hair off my head with his pocket knife. He was breathing fast as if he had been running hard. I began to tremble from head to foot and a pounding in my head and
throbbing in my chest nearly made me burst, but something inside told me to pretend I was still asleep. After
he took my curl he walked softly away and disappeared
forward. I never let Nelson learn that I knew what he
had done. Somehow I felt it was a secret he wanted to
keep. I began to keep away from Stitches and Father.
I just wanted to hide where no one could see how I felt.

Nelson never acted as though he had cut off my hair
that quiet night. A few days later I heard him telling
Swede and Bulgar his ambition as the three of them sat
whittling sticks in the scupper near the mizzen mast.

"I stuck by this barge 'cause I'm workin' for a job

of second mate. Ever since I left the old country I been
plannin' to get officer's papers," he said.

"There ain't nothin' in being a second mate. Responsibility at sea and standin' watch in port. Not for me!"
volunteered Swede with all the contempt in his voice he
could master.

"Some day I'll have a ship of my own," went on Nelson, "and she'll be the fastest full-rigger afloat."

"You mean you're going to be a Captain Nelson?" I
asked. He looked straight at me. Again I felt my face
flush hotly. "Yes, and there ain't going to be no women-
kind on my ship when I'm Skipper. Women belongs on
land," he answered.

I couldn't stand it, I fled aft and hid again—away from
myself.

"What are you moping around about, Joan?" Father
asked me that night. "Lately you been pale as a white
squall, and so quiet you must be sick. What's the matter
with you?"

"Nothing—except that I wish I was a million miles
away from here. I wish I was never on a ship. I wish I
was on land!" I cried at him.

"I set you ashore once and you ran away, so now I
ain't going to let you go navigatin' on the land until
you can steer a clear course. I seen too much of what livin' ashore does to women,—it fills their heads so full of
ballast that real cargoes such as common sense haven't
got any place. I'll not cast off your hawsers from the
ship until you can sail in fair or foul weather by yourself without runnin' aground." Those were the only
words of warning my father gave me, and I don't know to
this day if he knew the turmoil I was in. If he suspected

I was in love he didn't let me know it! We arrived in
Newcastle, Australia, a few weeks later. As usual, the
crew went ashore after the long sea trip, to frequent the
pubs along the waterfront. The second mate got in a
drunken brawl and was put in jail. Swede, Bulgar and
Oleson just kept away without reporting for duty for a
week. One day Father left the ship early in the morning
to attend to chartering a cargo of coal and left me on
board. We were anchored out in the channel. The only
others on the ship were the Jap cook, Stitches, and Fred
Nelson.

"You're the most sober man I got, Nelson," Father
said. "You take the day shift of watchman while I'm
ashore."

"Yes, sir," came back Nelson, pleased that Father had
noticed his sobriety. It would stand him in good stead
when he came up for a second mate's license.

Along about noon I got so lonesome for someone to
talk to that I sought out Nelson. I found him down in
the hold of the ship coiling up ropes and otherwise cleaning the hold ready for its next cargo. I slid down a rope
to the keel. Nelson didn't even speak to me, so I asked:

"Can I watch you work, Nelson?"

"You're the Skipper's daughter, so I suppose you can
do anything you damn please," was his unpromising answer.

I sat down on a big coil of rope and let my feet hang
over but they didn't quite reach the floor of the hold.
For perhaps half an hour I sat there. I was thinking.
Nelson was working. Neither of us said a word. All of a
sudden Nelson turned quickly towards me and before I
could realize what was happening he grabbed me and

kissed me! My head swam. I felt dizzy. I was thrilled and frightened. All in a confused instant the thought that I was bad because I liked that kiss stabbed my consciousness. I wanted to run from the hold up to the sunlight, but I couldn't move. My first grown-up kiss from a man! If only the bottom of the ship would open and swallow me.

From what seemed miles away I heard Nelson's voice speaking to me. He had walked back to his chore of cleaning and from there he said:

"How did you like that one, huh? That was just what you was aching for, wasn't it?"

So he blasted my illusion. For that kiss *was* just what I had been aching for but I could have killed him for putting my thought into words.

Through a daze I heard him continue:

"You better not tell the Old Man I kissed you. He'd raise hell with me."

I had no intention of telling Father about that kiss. I climbed out of the hold to the deck. I felt that every one would see when they looked at me that I had been kissed for I thought that kiss stuck out like a flaming mushroom on my face.

When Father returned to the ship that night he looked at me and didn't see anything wrong.

Long days of loading on coal passed, but I avoided going on deck when I knew Nelson would be on duty. How I treasured that kiss! Each morning when I washed my face I was careful to leave untouched the portion the kiss was on, with the result that my countenance gave the effect of a clean swept beach with a dark circle left by a receding tide in the region of my mouth. I was preserving as precious that kissed spot because how did I know I would ever get another one.

My happiness was complete until my father got a good look at my face while we sat at the dining table. The reflected light from the skylight overhead betrayed me. Father saw my dirty face.

"What do you mean by coming to the table without washing your face?" he demanded. I never thought so fast for an excuse in my life.

"I can't wash around my mouth, Father, because it's all chapped and it's too sore."

Father rose from the table, clutched me by the suspenders of my overalls and propelled me to the sink in the pantry. "Too sore to wash, huh?" he said and he took some sandsoap (the kind used to scrub down the decks) and a rag. With them he wiped the kiss, or what was left of it, from my face forever. I think in that moment I felt I suffered my greatest tragedy. I didn't want to see Nelson again for fear he would think I wanted him to kiss me again. I did want him to, that's why I avoided him.

When the cargo was loaded Father went ashore to bail his crew out of jail. He found all of them except the second mate willing to come back and ship out. The second mate refused to be bailed, and it put Father in a hole because officers for American ships are difficult to get in a foreign port.

"Why don't you make Nelson second mate?" I ventured to Father when I heard him grumbling about his bad luck with crews. The idea appealed to him, for he said to the first mate:

"Send Nelson aft to me, Mr. Owens."

I was delighted. If Nelson was made an officer I would

see him every day at the table. We would eat together —oh, the thrill of that thought! To eat with him three times a day for a six months' voyage! I could be friends with a second mate, according to Father's code of discipline, but not with a common sailor.

Nelson came into Father's quarters very much ill at ease.

"Yes sir, Captain. You sent for me, sir?"

"I'm going to ship you out as second mate. If you make good from here to Adelaide, I'll indorse your license for Officer's papers. Get your sea bag aft, at once. Your duty begins now," and Father turned to his bills of lading as the way of dismissing the conversation.

I stood near grinning, I was so happy. I saw Nelson's face flush bright red. He looked at Father. Then he looked at me and back at Father again. The flush had gone out of his face and his mouth made a straight line.

"I have to refuse, Captain. I don't want to be a second mate. I'd like my discharge, sir," Nelson said, almost defensively.

Father turned on him as if he hadn't heard him rightly.

"Are you a damned fool or just plain crazy? What do you mean, 'don't want to be a mate?' "

"That's it, sir. I'd like to be discharged," came back Nelson. My heart sank. Why did he want to leave? It was the dream of his life to be an officer and he was throwing away his first chance.

"Then get the hell off this ship and not a damned cent of pay will you get!" bellowed Father at him. Nelson left the cabin. I followed him, and ran after him. I caught up to him and pulled his arm to hold him back.

"Why are you going to leave, Nelson?"

Nelson took me by the shoulders and shook me. I was crying and I didn't try to hide my tears. It was the first time any sailor had seen me bawl but I wasn't ashamed. The awful fear—the ghastly loneliness of the prospect of losing Nelson—gripped me.

"Aw, what the hell, Skipper. If I stay on this ship as second mate I'd be seeing you every day, three times a day, even at meal times.

"An' if I was to be near to you like that every day I'd be makin' love to you, see?"

"But isn't that what you would want?" I asked, for it certainly was what I wanted—what I dreamed of.

"Sure, Skipper, but being so close like to you, this packet wouldn't be big enough for us both. You never had a chance—why, you ain't growed up yet, and any man'd be a dog to make love to a baby like you."

With those words Nelson turned from me and walked forward in great haste.

The next morning he went over the gangplank with his sea bag without looking back even to wave good-bye to me as I stood in the rigging watching him go. That was the last time I ever set eyes on Nelson. I have learned since that he was killed in a race riot on the docks in Galveston.

Of course I know that land folks would think Nelson a fool—a dear, chivalrous fool. Maybe—but I'll never forget him.

21

"You pull for the shore, boys,
Praying to Heaven above,
But I'll go down in the angry deep
With the ship I love."

WITH the red of the ship's waterline weighted deep in the water we sailed from Newcastle with a cargo of coal. Father shipped a new man in place of Nelson, a John Johnson. Father could have shipped a thousand sailors but none of them would fill the place in my life that Nelson did. John Johnson was a bully second mate and he handled his watch with an iron hand, but when off duty he was as gentle as the down on an albatross's wing. Johnson had great difficulty with his pronunciation of "J." His Norwegian origin was very obvious.

"Are you a Dane?" I asked him the second day out. I hoped he would say yes, because then he could in a way remind me of Nelson.

"I bane no Dane. I am Norwegian," he boasted. His accent was so marked that the crew used to sing when he was out of their hearing:

"Yumping Yimminy!
Yacob yumped off the Yib Boom with his
monkey yacket on. Yeesus! What a Yump!"

We sailed for weeks and June found us in the tropics. June is the hurricane season in the South Seas when freak storms, baffling winds and dangerous currents menace seafarers.

Father was on watch almost constantly at night. He would make frequent trips to his cabin to watch the barometer, only to return to the deck and pace up and down.

"Are we going to nose into a blow?" I asked Father.

"There's more than a blow going to strike us, Joan. I got a feeling in my marrow that we're a-headin' for our last anchorage," he said. Father, like all men of the deep sea, was superstitious, but, of course, when accused he denied it vigorously. The crew of a ship are guided by the Captain. If the Captain grows restless and worried the men suspect that he has gotten wind of impending disaster. What it is about the sea that whispers warnings to those who battle it I don't know, but that there is something, I am sure.

"There's a Jonah on this vessel." Father spit the words out to the mate on watch. The mate cast a suspicious glance at Bulgar, who was at the helm.

"It ain't him," Father said with finality. Bulgar heard the discussion but he appeared to be oblivious to it. He just went on chewing his wad of tobacco and spitting with unerring accuracy into the codfish keg near the wheel. Occasionally he lifted his eyes from the compass to watch the full spread of wind-taut sail. The topsails were set and pulling, and when the weather permits topsails it is a sign of fair wind.

The mate had no patience with Father's fears.

"There ain't nothin' to jaw about with this fair wind, Cap'n," he argued. "We had a good trip so far. Only one man, that Swede, had to be put in irons for trying to kill the cook."

Swede had caught the cook in the act of putting a dead cat into the slumgullion, as ship stew is termed. Cook was holding out the salt beef for himself and pawning off dead pussy. Taking fo'c's'le justice in his own hands Swede caught Cook by the back of the neck and began to shake the liver out of him. The cook managed to get his meat cleaver and attempted to assassinate Swede. There would have been a dual murder in the galley if Bulgar and Oleson hadn't intervened in time. Father put Swede in irons for attempted murder, but we needed the cook, so all that happened to him for bad conduct was forfeiture of one month's pay.

"Been nothin' but trouble ever since we sailed from Newcastle. Two men at the pumps night and day to keep down the water leakin' in the hold. Fights in the fo'c's'le. Joan not eating, and I been dreamin' about a broken anchor."

To make matters worse a large rat came up on deck one night shortly after that, looking for water. I tried to catch it to play with. I chased it off the poop deck, down the main deck and into the scupper. I had it cornered behind a rain barrel and was just about to grab its tail when it darted back into the scupper. In its fright it ran out a hawse hole and fell into the sea.

"My old rat got away from me, Stitches," I confided. Stitches was aghast with fear.

"Did a rat leave the ship?"

"No, I chased him overboard," I answered.

"Don't you tell your Old Man a rat left the ship. He's like a seethin' volcano now, ready to erupt 'cause he can't lay his finger on trouble he smells in the wind," Stitches warned me.

Despite Father's fears we reached the island of Rurutu, discharged the coal there, picked up a load of sandalwood and cat's eyes for a deck load after we had collected nine hundred tons of copra and sailed for Adelaide, South Australia, our destination.

The mate, cocky about the ship-shape condition of the vessel under his supervision, reminded Father of his groundless fears on the out trip.

"But we ain't in home port yet," Father persisted.

So he kept up his vigil. After seventy-one days we were due to sight land if Father's navigation was correct. Sailors were stationed at the masthead and on the bow as lookouts.

"Land off the starboard bow, ho!" wailed Swede from his post at the foremast crosstrees.

"Where away?" returned Father.

"Quarter point off the bow, sir!"

Sighting land after seventy-one weary days at sea was a great relief to Father. He hurried below, after giving a direction to the man at the wheel, and brought up his binoculars. He gazed steadily through them as if he were trying to bring the land closer through the glasses.

"That's it! Take a look, Joan."

Through the glasses I saw a little cone-shaped shadow on the horizon. Land!

"It's the sou'east point of Australia," opined Father. He climbed half way up the rigging of the spanker mast and clung to the ratlines. "We'll hit Bass Straits tonight!"

Then Father slid down the rigging to the deck and spoke to the mate:

"The Straits are a helluva passage to make at night. There's no moon out to navigate by. All hands on deck —stand by."

Although the Straits are one hundred miles across, that leaves little room for a sailing ship to beat and tack in. There is a channel of deep water running through the center of the Straits where the currents are less deadly. The sweep of the Pacific meets the rushing tides of the Indian Ocean. Mountainous promontories rise on the coast of South Australia and the jutting saw-toothed coast of Tasmania guards the southern end of the straits. Baffling winds and treacherous cross-currents stirred by the vortex of waters from three oceans, the Pacific, Indian and Antarctic meeting, make sailing dangerous. Sometimes the wind dies suddenly shut off by a mountain range only to kick up again in a fury from an opposite direction. It is no feat at all for steam vessels to go through the Straits but a sailing ship is at the mercy of the winds and tides.

Almost like magic the land loomed larger and larger, until the blue haze faded and we could distinguish

Wilson Promontory. It looked like a huge whale asleep on the water. It was about four bells in the evening and the tropic light was rapidly fading into a soft gray.

"Clew in the topsails! Sheet home the jibs!" called Father suddenly. It isn't just duty that makes sailors over-eager to hasten a ship's arrival in port. They are contented until they sight land and then they become restless.

"A sailorman can sniff a drink in the wind a hundred miles out to sea," Stitches declared.

In less than five minutes the topsails were fast and only the flying jib was set. Father went aloft with his binoculars. Far off to leeward I saw a vermilion-colored light-ship jerking at its anchorage near the shore.

Eight bells struck! The watch changed. The moaning of buoys came out of the darkness to warn us of reefs and shallow water.

I ascended the mast to be near Father.

"You turn in, Joan. If any trouble comes, keep out of the way, do you hear?"

"Yes, sir!" I replied, for when he used that tone to me "Yes, sir" was the only thing to say. I stuck my head out of my porthole watching the phosphorus in the water make the sea look as if it were on fire until I became too sleepy to sit up. I got my family of cats from the chart-room and put them under the blankets at my feet. Under the covers their eyes looked just as the phosphorus in the water did. I mention those kittens because they played a big part in the "trouble" Father had predicted. He had always forbidden me to take the cats into my bunk.

"Bedbugs and cockroaches can't be avoided in bunks but cats can be, so don't you let me catch you taking them to bed with you."

I put my own interpretation on that advice. I couldn't catch the bedbugs and roaches but I could catch the cats. I kept them under the covers so their protesting meowing wouldn't reach Father's ears. Then I fell sound asleep. I was wakened by a heavy rain squall and stiff wind which shook the ship. I lay in my bunk listening to the seas slap the porthole above me. I heard Father shouting above the wind to the crew, and faintly the answering calls of men came back. Shallow water when it becomes rough rocks a ship unlike a deep sea storm. The difference in the rolling made me peer out the porthole. A sudden jolt of the ship threw me flat on the bunk. If only that wind would blow steadily and not in jerks—but I was asleep before I could form any more opinions.

I don't know how long I was asleep before I awoke in a fit of coughing. My eyes burned. I rubbed them with my fist but they watered and stung more. I quit rubbing them but they hurt even more and then I could hardly breathe. It was pitch dark in my cabin and I thought I was having a nightmare. My senses began to dim and I felt as if I were going a long way off from my body. The scuffling of feet on the poop deck—hoarse shouts—confusion, then a cry that pierced my dulled brain sent a chill of fear through me.

"Fire!"

"Fire! Fire!" The words were repeated and echoed hollowly in the wind. "Fire!" That was what I was thinking the phosphorus in the sea looked like. I tried to wake up. Surely I was dreaming.

"It's in the after hold."

"The paint locker is burning!"

I couldn't move from my bunk for I was paralyzed with fear. Over and over in my fast dimming consciousness I could hear "Paint Locker." "FIRE!" The curses of the men above grew faint. I could feel the kittens scratching under the covers at my feet to get out but I could make no effort to help them. Had there been a light in my cabin I would have seen the dense smoke choking the air—slowly suffocating me. Why couldn't I move? Why didn't some one help me? But too well I knew the code of the sea that reckons one life as little where the safety of the ship is concerned.

The floors of the cabin were caulked with tar and oakum. Fire from below had burned the underpinnings and the tar was boiling in the cracks.

On deck Father opened the lazarette hatch and flames six feet high burst out. The cargo of copra in the hold was a blazing inferno! Copra is highly explosive. The rubbing and grating of the stuff in the freak storm had caused spontaneous combustion. The flames licked up from out the open hatch and overcame the mate. Father's face was burned, and his hands blistered. The wind swept down into the hold and fanned the fire into a vicious furnace.

I finally managed to get out of my bunk and found my way by groping through the smoke to the chartroom. I could smell where the companionway was by the rush of fresh air that poured down from it. But the air only served to fan the gasping licks of fire that had eaten up through the cabin floor into a blaze. I tried to reach the companionway door. Clad only in a flour-sack nightgown and in my bare feet I picked my way over the hot tar on the floor to the ladder leading to the deck. Then I remembered the kittens I had left to smother under the covers in my bunk.

I felt my way back to the cabin and blindly reached for them. I found them huddled in the farthest corner of the bunk. The ship gave a sudden toss and sent me sprawling to the floor with my arm full of kittens. They dug their claws into my bare flesh and held on. I tried to get back to the companionway, but the fire had eaten through from below. I stood on the edge of the chart-room unable to go farther. My feet were burned and the pain was almost more than I could bear. The smoke choked me. It stung and burned my eyes. The kittens were clawing at the raw flesh around my breasts.

The realization that I was going to die seemed a relief. I became calm. If I died, the terrible pain would stop. I stood perfectly still, just waiting, for I couldn't move another step.

On deck pandemonium had broken loose. The sails slapped and ripped. The deserted helm spun dizzily around leaving the ship at the mercy of the choppy sea. Then, from what seemed millions of miles away, I heard an agonized cry. I recognized the voice of Stitches:

"JOAN?"

I tried to answer him, but all I could manage was a whispered, "Here I am."

"Joan! Skipper! Where are you?"

Oh, wouldn't he ever find me! I couldn't help myself. Smoke and pain and panic overcame me. I couldn't speak another word. I heard his voice coming nearer—and then a numbness crept over me so that I hardly knew what was happening. Stitches came down the companionway from the forward entrance and into the dining saloon. Finally his arms found me and my cats. Picking me up in his old arms he carried me over and out of the fire which was licking up in scarlet tongues of flame all over the deck of the cabins.

Just as he reached the top of the companionway ladder Stitches dropped with a gasp under me. We struck the deck and lay there side by side. Then the sight of the sky, the wind and rain on my face, the fresh air in my lungs brought me to. I staggered to my feet, and bending over tried to arouse Stitches. He was dead! He had crowned the years of his devotion by giving his life to save mine. He had done his job the best he knew how and he would go under the waves with his ship for his coffin—a sailorman found his last anchorage! No matter how long I live Stitches will be a memory of the sea that nothing will erase.

I could see they were lowering the lifeboat off the stern. I caught Stitches' body under the arms and tried to drag it to the poop deck. Swede saw me.

Rushing over he jerked me from Stitches, dragged me to the poop deck and flung me into the lifeboat.

On the poop deck by the spanker mast were two kegs of gasoline used for starting the donkey engine forward to hoist cargo in port. They were lashed to the deck with chains. If the fire reached them the ship and every one on board would be blown to bits. They were lashed too securely to be chopped away in time to save them from the fire which had already eaten through to the poop. There wasn't a second to be lost.

"Pull away to leeward, then head for the lightship,"

shouted Father. He didn't even stop to see if his command was carried out. He and the mate and two of the sailors were bailing up canvas bucket after canvas bucket of sea water to throw on the fire.

The ship began to fill with water from the open scuttles. The weight of the sea water in the hold sank the vessel deeper, but it forced the fire up through the decks. The *Minnie A. Caine* wallowed like a stricken thing under the vast weight of water. I worked back to a place in the stern of the dinghy. Then I discovered the cats were still clinging to me. Afterwards I found they had sunk their claws deep in my flesh. At the time I scarcely noticed the pain.

Father and the mate stayed on the poop deck until the burning vessel sunk to the water line when they plunged overboard, jumping clear of the hull. The ship tossed by a big swell capsized over on its beam ends. A hissing, bubbling sound came from her as the flames were buried in the sea. Father and the mate swam to the lifeboat which was leaking badly. The tropic heat had warped the seams in it and it was filling faster than we could bail it out. The rain, the spray from the waves and the thick smoke from the smothered fire made vision impossible. I could barely see the other figures in the lifeboat. The men pulled long strokes towards the shore.

We were about a hundred yards away from the ship and through the maze of smoke all we could see were the topmasts sticking above the sea. The wind was freezing and the cold rain wet us through and through. My nightgown was poor protection against the wind and water, but I was so terrified I wasn't conscious that I was nearly freezing.

"Pull! Pull! PULL!" Father's voice set the heat for the men at the oars.

"Are all hands here?" he asked. Swede, Bulgar, Oleson, the mate, cabin-boy, Johnson and me were the only ones to answer the roll call. The Jap cook had jumped overboard and failed to make the lifeboat. Stitches' charred body was somewhere cradled in the burnt hull of the ship. Over the roar of the wind and rain the buoys kept up their monotonous warnings—and shorewards the riding light of the light ship traced semi-circles against the sky as her masts rolled heavily in the onshore breakers. We were about a quarter mile away from the wreck when the smoke cleared. Father gazed back at his ship, which looked like some glorious living thing struck dead. It was too much for Father to endure. With a gurgling sound of agony in his throat he pulled in his oar:

"O Christ!" I heard him gasp. Then he stood up, trying to plunge into the sea and return to his beloved ship. Only the strong restraining arms of Swede and Oleson kept him back. He struggled like a maniac.

"Let me go, you ——s. Let me go!" he cried.

In this crisis the mate, Johnson, saved Father and us.

"The lifeboat's sinking, Captain," he said.

Those words brought Father out of his frenzy of grief at losing his ship. For the first time in my life I saw Father cry. He covered his eyes with his hands as if to shut out the sight. The weight of our bodies in the life boat opened up the already leaking seams.

Father reached through the rain to where I crouched in the stern and grabbed my arm. In a voice that became suddenly calm—he was once more the master in command, he said:

"Joan! Swim for it, kid,—the lightship." He pointed to the pin point of light which was about three miles away. "Swim slowly and high out of water. And breathe deep, Joan, as deep as you can."

"Yes, sir!" I answered, trying to hide the terror of the long swim.

"If you get all in—float. Take it easy, girl. I'll be right behind you."

He had only time to finish those words when the lifeboat filled with water up to the gunwales. If I had to swim no nightgown was going to get in my way to drag me down. I tore it from me, but the drenched kittens still clung to my flesh. I filled my lungs with a deep breath and jumped out of the lifeboat. When I came up in the choppy sea I was conscious of only the pain caused by the salt water on my bleeding cuts and scratches. Each stroke I took was like a knife cut, and I couldn't shake the drowning kittens off. Perhaps to those cats I owe my life, for the pain made me so mad I fought on and on, toward the lightship which seemed to go farther away instead of closer. I could hear the others swimming near me, just the "cut-splash—cut-splash!" of their strokes. I had swum about a mile against a high running sea with the cats on my back. I was exhausted, so I trod water and drank the fresh rain that poured down. That is a trick for deep sea swimming—to drink rain water which absorbs the salt water that is swallowed.

Two of the men, Swede and Johnson, were ahead of me. Swede began a song. It was his bravery, his daring to sing in the face of near death that put courage into me. If Swede could sing then I could hold out too, for wasn't I a regular sailor, and here was a supreme test.

I plowed on through the seas. I thought I had been swimming hours, when Father's voice a few yards abreast me called:

"Just ahead now—there she looms!"

That was all I remembered until the next morning at daybreak. I came to on the iron deck of the lightship with only a man's vest on my naked torn body. A strange man was bending over me. He turned out to be the keeper of the lightship.

"She must be a damn fine swimmer because young things is hard to kill."

He lifted me off the deck and carried me to his warm cabin where I lost consciousness again. The cats were gone! Somewhere in that last quarter mile they were lost.

Late that afternoon I awoke. The engineer of the lightship gave me a warm suit of dungarees and a heavy sweater to wear, and then we learned what had happened. The look-out on the lightship had seen the fire on board. He attempted to launch a small boat to come to rescue us when the Southerly Buster squall arose and made the feat impossible. He and his men watched from the crow's nest on the mast all night through. They saw the ship capsize. Through powerful binoculars they scanned the sea for a sign of us in our lifeboat. At almost daybreak Swede and Oleson reached the lightship, then followed Johnson, the cabin-boy and Bulgar. Swede swam back to get me and he dragged my limp body to the lightship. The lightship keeper threw over a running bowline which Swede made fast around my stomach and back and they hoisted me on deck. Father and the mate were the last to be pulled aboard.

We stayed on the lightship for three days. Father couldn't speak. He stood by the rail for hours at a time just staring out towards the sea. He refused food. I tried to talk with him but he didn't hear me.

"From a skipper to a bum!—I'm through forever now," he finally said, more to the sea than to any person, as the Government cutter from Melbourne steamed alongside the light ship to take us ashore, in answer to the S.O.S. call sent by the lightship Keeper.

And Father *was* through too. The day of steam ships has come. Old sailing captains have no place any longer. My father was seventy years old, and broken by the wreck. He is living ashore now, near the coast on the Pacific, but his spirit is not on the land—it is far off in the tropics dreaming of a fair wind and the stars of the Southern Cross to steer a course by.

CPSIA information can be obtained
at www.ICGtesting.com
Printed in the USA
LVHW010857281018
595121LV00010B/447/P